LO · VE
樂府

心里满了，就从口中溢出

Alexis Wright

Odyssey of the Horizon

〈地平線の叙事詩〉

地平线上的奥德赛

[澳] 亚历克西斯 · 赖特 著
李尧 [日] 有满保江 译

北京联合出版公司
Beijing United Publishing Co.,Ltd

目录
Contents
目次

序言

在亚历克西斯·赖特的作品中，我们可以听到许多声音。她以不同的形式讲述故事，把过去、现在以及未来的愿景糅合在一起。故事里有幽默与悲伤，希望与绝望，壮丽与亲密，诗歌与政治。她让我们听到祖先的声音，听到她和我们同时代人的声音：痛苦的沉默，抗议的呼声，表现力量的歌声。

那是一条漫长的道路。25 年的文学生涯中，赖特出版了三部获奖小说：《希望的平原》（1997）、《卡彭塔利亚湾》（2006）和《天鹅书》（2013）。还有三部重要的虚构作品《格罗格酒之战》（1997）、《像这位老人一样夺取权力》（1998）、《追踪者》（2017）和许多短篇小说、散文。《卡彭塔利亚湾》获 2007 年迈尔斯·富兰克林文学奖，《追踪者》获 2018 年斯特拉奖。这两个奖项都是澳大利亚最高文学奖。她的作品涉猎极广。每一部新作品，都创造出一种独特的形式和风格表达她的思想。她是今日之世界为数不多的、能够用自己的语言讲述“穿越无数个千年……流传下来的”她的国家的故事的作家之一，并且在社会和全球陷入危机，我们共同面临困境的时刻，展示这些故事的意义和价值。

亚历克西斯·赖特是一名来自澳大利亚北部卡彭塔利亚湾南部的瓦伊族妇女。1950 年，她出生于昆士兰的克朗克里，后来在澳大利亚中部的艾丽斯·斯普林斯生活多年。在那里，她作为一名为原住民权利而斗争的社会活动家和组织者辛勤工作。亚历克西斯·赖特现居住在墨尔本，其作品被翻译成多种语言，包括中文。2012 年，诺贝尔文学奖得主莫言发布了由李尧翻译的《卡彭塔利亚湾》。

赖特解释说，她讲的故事“与土著世界有关……(推动)穿越边界，描述一个复杂的家园，里面有许多思想和精神的精髓”。她的灵感来自世界各地的作家，比如爱尔兰诗人谢默斯·希尼（Seamus Heaney）、匈牙利小说家拉兹洛·克拉斯纳霍卡伊（László Krasznahorkai）、拉丁美洲作家卡洛斯·富恩特斯（Carlos Fuentes）和爱德华多·加莱亚诺（Eduardo Galeano），还有来自马提尼克岛的帕特里克·查莫伊索（Patrick Chamoisseau）和爱德华·格里森特（Edouard Glissant），以及阿拉伯国家、中国和日本的作家。她汲取、融合了世界文学精华，并为之做出重大贡献。

亚历克西斯·赖特的作品体现了祖先过去至高无上的地位。读她的作品，我们对长者的尊敬油然而生。这些故事极具感染力，对当代和未来一代代人们——无论原住民还是非原住民——都是宝贵财富，也是不断的源泉。

《地平线上的奥德赛》是亚历克西斯·赖特的新作，对于刚开始读她作品的读者，是一个很好的起点。这本书以英文、日文、中文合集的形式出版，日文和中文译者是我的朋友有满保江和李尧。《地平线上的奥德赛》是寓言，是散文，也是诗。这部作品是为了回应视觉艺术家特雷西·莫法特在 2017 年威尼斯双年展上的作品《我的地平线》而创作的。《地平线上的奥德赛》由赖特的女儿莉莉·萨文克担任美术设计。这种合作是赖特向我们展示的关于历史令人心灵震颤的美的一部分。在一系列六个相互关联的章节中，她的散文将多个时间段结合在一起，将形象与情感紧密地糅合在一起，描绘了 1788 年英国“幽灵船”穿越地平线，入侵悉尼湾的那一刻；描绘了故事中的古老时代“……持续不断地被‘看护’这个‘故事国家’的人重复”；描绘了暴力殖民创伤性记忆层层叠叠“深入未来几代人的噩梦”以及“世界历史上数以百万计饱受战争摧残的人”的迁徙，包括今天在澳大利亚寻找新家的无名难民儿童。这些经历在赖特的散文中相互交织，在诗歌和故事的蒙太奇中不断重叠，密不可分。作者所说的“历史的悲哀”在人类的神话中回荡，就像古希腊诗人荷马的《奥德赛》在 21 世纪依然延续。

我很高兴在这篇简短的序言中向读者介绍这位重要作家的作品。《地平线上的奥德赛》会带给你一种非常有益的阅读体验。听听亚力克西斯 · 赖特是怎么说的吧。

尼古拉斯 · 周思

2019 年 10 月 1 日

Preface

Many voices can be heard in the work of Alexis Wright. Her storytelling takes different forms as she brings past time together with present time and with visions of the future. There is humour and sorrow, hope and despair, grandeur and intimacy, poetry and politics. She lets us hear the voices of her ancestors and the voices of her—and our—contemporaries: the silence of suffering, the cry of protest, the song of strength.

It has been a long journey. In a career of 25 years, Wright has published three award-winning novels *Plains of Promise* (1997), *Carpentaria* (2006) and *The Swan Book* (2013), three major works of non-fiction, *Grog War* (1997), *Take Power Like This Old Man Here* (1998) and *Tracker* (2017), and many short stories and essays. *Carpentaria* won the Miles Franklin Literary Award in 2007 and *Tracker* won the Stella Prize in 2018, two of Australia's top literary awards. Her writing has an extraordinary range . With each new work she creates a unique form and style to express her ideas. She is one of the few writers at work in the world today who can tell the stories of her country as they have been 'passed down ... through countless millennia', in her words, and show us their meaning and value for the predicament we face together at a time of community and global crisis.

Alexis Wright is a Waanyi woman from the southern Gulf of Carpentaria in Northern Australia. She was born in Cloncurry, Queensland, in 1950. Later she lived in Alice Springs in Central Australia for many years where she worked as an activist and organiser for Aboriginal rights. She now lives in Melbourne. Her work has been translated into many languages, including Chinese, where the translation of *Carpentaria* by Li Yao was launched by Mo Yan, the Nobel literature laureate, in 2012.

Wright explains that she tells 'stories that relate to the Aboriginal world... [pushing] through boundaries to describe a complex home with many geographies of the mind and spirit'. She is inspired by writers from all around the world—the Irish poet Seamus Heaney, for example, and the Hungarian novelist Laszlo Krasznahorkai, Latin American writers such as Carlos Fuentes and Eduardo Galeano, and Patrick Chamoisseau and Edouard Glissant from Martinique, and other writers in Arabic, Chinese and Japanese. She draws on the literature of the world in solidarity and makes her own significant contribution to it.

Alexis Wright's body of work speaks from the authority of the ancestral past. We honour the elders as we read her work. It speaks with powerful agency to the present and for future generations, Indigenous and non-Indigenous alike, it is a treasure and a resource.

Odyssey of the horizon is a new work by Alexis Wright and a good place for new readers to start. It is published here in Japanese and Chinese, translated by my friends Yasue Arimitsu and Li Yao. Part fable, part essay, part poem, *Odyssey of the horizon* was created in response to the work of visual artist Tracey Moffatt called *My Horizon,* made for the 2017 Venice Biennale. This book is designed by Wright's daughter Lily Sawenko. Its collaborative nature is part of the beauty of the moving and disturbing riff on history that Wright gives us. In a series of six linked sections, her prose brings multiple time periods together in a powerful fusion of image and emotion: the moment when the British 'ghost ships' of invasion come across the horizon at Sydney Cove in 1788, the ancient time of story, 'continuously renewed ... by the caretakers of their story country', the traumatic layered memories of colonial violence, carried 'far into the dreams of the generations to come', and the movement of 'millions of other war-torn people in the history of the world', including nameless refugee children who today seek a new home in Australia. These experiences are inextricably linked as they flow together in Wright's prose, overlapping in a montage of poetry and story. What the author calls 'the history sadness' echoes through the myths of humanity, as the unending *Odyssey* of the old Greek poet Homer continues in the twenty-first century.

It is my pleasure in this short preface to introduce readers to the work of this important writer. *Odyssey of the horizon* is a richly rewarding reading experience. Listen to what Alexis Wright has to say.

Nicholas Jose
October 1, 2019

序文

アレクシス・ライト著、『地平線の叙事詩』（*Odyssey of the Horizon*）という作品からは、さまざまな声が聞こえてくる。この物語の語りは、ライトならではの独特な形式で書かれている。まずこの作品では、過去の時間と未来の時間がともに、現在の時間の中に取り込まれている。作品にはユーモアと悲哀、希望と絶望、壮麗さと親密さ、詩と政治などが織り交ぜられ描かれている。著者は我われ読者に、先住民である彼女の先祖たちの声を、また彼女自身の声を、そして現代に生きる我われすべての人間の声を聞かせてくれる。読者はその声の中に、声にならない苦悩、抵抗の叫び声、力強い歌を聞きとることができるのである。

それはとても長い旅だった。彼女の作家としてのキャリアは25年ほどだが、その間に3冊の主要な小説、*Plains of Promise*『約束の土地』(1997)、*Carpentaria*『カーペンタリア』(2006)、そして *The Swan Book*『スワン・ブック』(2013) を出版している。また3冊の主要なノンフィクションの作品、*Grog War*『グロッグ戦争』(1997)、*Take Power Like This Old Man Here*『天下を取れ、この地のこの老人のように』(1998)、そして *Tracker*『追跡者』(2017) を出版し、その他の多くの短編やエッセイも世に出している。『カーペンタリア』は2007年にマイルズ・フランクリン賞を受賞、『追跡者』は2018年にステラ賞を受賞している。これらの賞はオーストラリアのトップクラスの文学賞である。彼女の作品は想像を絶するほど広範囲に及んでいる。また、彼女は新しい作品を書くたびに、自身の思想を表現するためのユニークな形式やスタイルを創り出している。彼女は現役の作家の中で、彼女が属する土地の物語を語ることのできる数少ない作家のひとりである。なぜならば、彼女が語っているのは、彼女のいう「数万年という途方もなく長い年月にわたって伝えられてきた」物語であり、その物語は共同体レベルと地球規模レベルの両方において、我われが直面する困難を乗り越えるための、非常に有益な意味や価値を示してくれるからである。

アレクシス・ライトは、北オーストラリアのカーペンタリア湾の南に位置する土地の、ワーニィ (Waanyi) 族に属する女性である。彼女は 1950 年にクィーンズランド州のクロンカリー (Cloncurry) に生まれた。後に中央オーストラリアのアリス・スプリングズに多年にわたって住み続け、先住民の権利獲得運動の活動家として、また社会運動家として行動してきた。現在はメルボルンに居住している。彼女の作品は、中国語を含め多くの言語に翻訳されており、ことに中国では『カーペンタリア』がリ・ヤオによって翻訳され、2012 年のノーベル文学賞受賞者であるモウ・ヤンによって世に送り出された。

ライトは『地平線の叙事詩』ついて、「この本は、アボリジナルの世界に関係した物語であり、精神と魂がさまざまな配列によって複雑な構造を成している故郷を描写するために、いろいろな境界線を突き破っている」と解説している。彼女は世界中の作家たちから影響を受けている。たとえばアイルランドの詩人、シェイマス・ヒーニー (Seamus Heaney)、ハンガリーの小説家、ラースロー・クラスナホルカイ (Laszlo Krasznahorkai)、ラテン・アメリカの作家、カルロス・フエンテス (Carlos Fuentes) やエドゥアルド・ガレアーノ (Eduardo Galeano)、そしてマルティニーク*出身のパトリック・シャモワゾー (Patrick Chamoisseau) やエドゥアール・グリッサン (Edouard Glissant)、その他、アラビア語、中国語、日本語を用いて作品を書く作家などからも影響を受けている。彼女の作品は、内容の統一性おいては世界文学に負うところが多く、彼女自身もまた作家として、世界文学へ重要な貢献をしている。

アレクシス・ライトの一連の作品は、先人たちの過去が典拠となっている。我われ読者は彼女の作品を読む時、彼女の先祖である長老たちに敬意を払う。ライトはその

* マルティニーク（Martinique）：西インド諸島南東部、Windward 諸島北部の島で、フランスの海外県。

先人たちと読者の間の力強い仲介役となり、先住民であろうとなかろうと、現代そして未来の世代のすべての人びとに向けて、先人たちの物語が宝物であり財産であることを伝えている。

『地平線の叙事詩』はアレクシス・ライトの最新の作品であり、彼女の作品を初めて読む読者にとってよいスタートになるであろう。この作品は日本語と中国語に翻訳され、しかも翻訳者は私の友人たちである、アリミツ・ヤスエ (Arimitsu Yasue) とリ・ヤオ (Li Yao) である。この作品は、あるときは伝説、あるときはエッセイ、またあるときは詩という形式をとっている。そもそもこの作品は、視覚芸術家であるトレイシー・モファット (Tracy Moffatt) が、2017 年にヴェニスで開催されたビエンナーレのために作成した『私の地平線』(*My Horizon*) という作品に応える形で創作されたものである。作品の表紙は、ライトのご令嬢でありグラフィック・デザイナーのリリー・ソウェンコ (Lily Sawenko) によってデザインされている。この作品の中でライトが語る歴史は、ときに読者を感動させ、ときに読者の心をかき乱すものであるが、それはリフ*に似た美を感じさせる。その美のある部分は、作品が共同制作であることから生まれるもので、この作品の特質ともなっている。彼女の散文は、六つの連結されたセクションの中で重層的な時間の周期を、イメージと感情の力強い融合によってひとつにまとめあげている。たとえば、英国の「幽霊船」が 1788 年にシドニー湾の水平線上に現れたとき、この物語の昔の時間では、「この土地に生まれた物語が、その物語を管理する人間たちによって継続的に新しく書き換えられて」おり、植民地時代に被った暴力に深く傷ついた彼らの記憶が何層にも重ねられ、次の世代の夢の中にも伝えられている。そして、「世界の歴史の中で引き裂かれた数百万人もの人びと」の行動も、その記憶の中に重ねられている。しかも、その中にはオーストラリアに新しい居住地を求めて訪れている名もない難民の子供

* リフ（riff）：ポピュラー音楽で、ソロ楽器やボーカルのバックとして使われる短い反復フレーズ。ブルースのテーマ部をいうこともある。

たちも含まれている。これら子供たちの経験は、ライトの散文の中で一緒に流れているように、異なる時代の異なる経験が決してほどけることなく複雑に絡みあい、さらには詩と物語という異なる形式が繫ぎあわされ重なりあっているのである。著者のいう「悲しい歴史」は、人間の神話や伝説を通してこだまのように繰り返され、それはあたかも古代ギリシャの詩人ホーマーの終わることのない叙事詩が、21 世紀にも継続されているかのようである。

この大変重要な作家の作品に読者を導いていく序文を書くことは、私にとってこの上ない喜びです。『地平線の叙事詩』は、必ず豊かな読書経験となることを確信しています。アレクシス・ライトが読者に語らなければならなかったことに、是非、耳を傾けていただきたい。

ニコラス・ジョーズ

2019 年 10 月 1 日

地平线上的奥德赛

〔澳〕亚历克西斯·赖特
李尧 译

古老的风

你看到的海浪将继续奔腾起伏，冲走想象中边疆的边界。强大的、时代的风暴侵蚀、摧毁了建造在我们心中、禁锢我们思想的壁垒，一如推翻钢筋和铁丝网建起的路障。洋流没有边界，它搅动了我们曾经触摸着想要抓鱼的水。没有什么能阻止生活在海浪下，被遗忘的神衡量我们意志的价值。我们的呼吸与别人的呼吸混合在一起，即使吹过这个地方的古老的风也总是在垃圾堆啸吟，演奏出交响乐，让所有人都能听到。

有一天，在维 - 荣，或者旺冉——属于这块土地南部陆地的达鲁人对悉尼湾的称谓——地平线上，白鬼打破了不属于他们的那块土地的边界。守卫海岸线的古老的风神吹过鬼船的每一个角落、每一道裂缝，闻到了死亡的臭气。她把脸贴在黏糊糊的船舷和囚犯肮脏苍白的皮肤上的时候，感觉到白鬼们的恐惧。那恐惧是显而易见、可以预知的。她往后一缩，像受了伤的动物，从恐惧中逃走。然后，像一个老阿姨一样，愤怒地尖叫着，冲过海浪，身后留下一道道白沫。她发了疯似的在海岸上跑来跑去，拽着云朵般迁徙的蝴蝶，在狂风怒号的海面上飞翔，试图清洁自己未受损伤的皮肤。

她在大陆上空的大气层盘旋了几千公里，散布有人入侵的消息。祖灵之首闻讯之后，掀起北旋风和风暴，撕裂了东海岸。天空中乌云密布，电闪雷鸣。生活在海浪下孔武有力的老祖宗吱吱嘎嘎摇晃着漂浮在海面的鬼船。那些船在波峰浪谷间颠簸，无法逃脱。但他们悄然无声，就像连一点精气神也没有的死了的东西。木头制作的船身对铸成这一方天地的创世老祖宗不肯放弃它们的精髓于万一。没有任何关于它们入侵的消息，老祖宗也没有听到别的什么声音，除了船钟发出叮叮当当的响声和一种闻所未闻的声音——不是神示，而是想要得到什么的呼喊。

这是一段长达八个月的史诗般的海上旅程。十一艘入侵的鬼船从遥远的不列颠尼亚[01]启航。那里的祖先神，比如被称为乌鸦的老国王神布兰[02]，教人们如何用剑统治。这些野蛮的征服者提着带血的鞭子，端着枪，在甲板上走来走去。古老的战神奴役人们的方式在他们的血液里有力地流淌。下面的货舱里，海神的儿子马纳南·麦克·利尔的海水也从许多囚犯的血管流过。

两个多世纪前的1788年1月26日，疾风鼓满巨大的白帆。木船上，有一千三百三十六个活生生的人。他们大多数是被关在拥挤不堪的船舱里的流放犯。这些可怜的人只是犯了无足轻重的罪，却被从家乡抓走，漂泊万里，送到地球的另一边，在皮鞭的逼迫下，为建立计划中的流放地而服苦役。他们遥远的政府和以英国女王的名义在这块大陆上建立的政府，都认为，而且仍将认为，这块土地无人居住。

因为这里的居民，哦，黑人！他们算什么人！

花了两个世纪的时间，那些步最初入侵者的后尘，踏上这块土地的人，才通过澳大利亚高等法院承认，占据这块大陆的传统的主人，是拥有世界上高度发达、精密复杂的古代律法和行政管理体系的民族之一。这些律法和管理体系使得这个国家作为一个整体运转，使其成为圣洁之地，成为世界上最大的法律“大教堂”，成为一座无与伦比的图书馆。它的知识通过远古以来的史诗故事储存在这块土地，并且由这块土地本身创造而来。这是一个几乎难以想象的巨大档案馆，通过人们与各式各样的自然景观的精神联系而受到关怀。

这些史诗般的故事是这块大陆法律的基础，在无数个千年里都被奉为神圣。并且在各种仪式上被他们的“故事国家”的管理者不断更新、阅读。这些有着崇高宗教信仰的“图书馆员”使得这种知识充满生命力，因为他们的后人还会从混沌之初讲起。但遗憾的是，对于传统的所有者来说，入侵从未停止，所有可怕的后果一直持续到今天。

想象一下白鬼的船到达时的情景。看到成百上千宛如鬼一样的人离开他们的船，踏上这块土地的沙滩时，达鲁人大为震惊。这些人对这个地方传统的律法故事的魅力全无兴趣，更无关系。即使按照今天世界人口的比例，突然之间一万一千个陌生人出现在你面前，也是一件让人惊讶不已的事情。达鲁人应该知道，白鬼的无知将使这块土地的精神陷入危险之中。

属于这块土地的人们

想象一下，当那些船只到达的时候，这块大陆传统的所有者从律法书浩如烟海的知识中知道多少关于治理他们土地的最古老的法律故事呢？他们从大地汲取知识，牢牢记在心中。由祖先创造并给予的指南，在世界上最悠久的文化中保存并代代相传。对于一个沉浸于那么多治理国家的古老知识的民族而言，任何变化都逃不过他们的眼睛。即使最微小的变化，比如水的流动，也能被发现，被破译。

这些第一次和白鬼接触的人中是否有一帮意志坚定的剽悍之徒曾经聚集在一起，争论不休，以便制定出保卫主权与边境的政策？是为一百万武士雕刻一百万支长矛，和入侵者决一死战，还是在这块土地周围筑一道石头墙，把自己关在里面，御敌于国门之外？或者，在旁边贫瘠的小岛建立几座离岸拘留营，把这些船民关起来，让他们在那里度过余生？不，祖先的故事指引的方向却不相同。老祖宗考虑问题的逻辑和行事的方法基于一直指引他们的法律故事。现在就要去做老祖宗可能会做的事情。寻求知识，相互理解，以维护古老的律法，保持国家的活力，防止它陷入危险之中。

老祖宗有着非常复杂精密的社会实践，这些实践把他们和这块土地这一部分的故事线连接到一起。在这里，律法指引他们前进。老人们来自一代代精通管理这块土地律法实践的哲人。他们领略过海浪起舞的壮美，熟知微风吹过的心情、蝴蝶翩翩的优雅；或者如何阅读先人留下的狂风暴雨的故事：飓风抽打豪雨，雨水拒绝落下。他们知道如何看大海，就如一直以来看它的行为方式和习惯。用他们经常表演的长长的连篇歌曲和它对话。解读经历无数个千年流传下来的故事中的符号。

这么说吧，咆哮的大海正被这块土地传统的所有者解读。也许白帆点点的大船到来的几天前，甚至几个月前，他们就已经知晓。“老妇人一定在哭，为何而哭呢？”他们或许谈论过这事儿。他们本应该知道，海风为什么在一年的这个时候吹来。因为他们和它的祖先关系密切。然而，这位至亲至爱的亲人却受到了打扰，行为举止变得古怪。他们以前从未听说过这样的事，即使狂风吹过风化的砂岩悬崖。在那里，你能听到对于这块土地而言非常重要的几个家族的呢喃细语，听到他们现在在哪儿宿营，等待不曾预料的事情发生，也许和从大地升腾而起的祖宗一起等待，天空俯瞰大海，而祖先们已经看到了白鬼。

他们可能已经感觉到入侵者骨子里的大恶，感觉到某种重要的生命本质正被一件异乎寻常的怪事从他们的身体里激发出来。焦躁不安的巨地鸠不停地发出节奏很快的咕咕声。然后，它们仿佛变成极度脆弱的影子人，体会在无尽的未来寻找并且最终找到灵魂的本质是什么滋味。年老的男人和妇人压低嗓门儿不停地和这块土地的精灵交谈，试图平息他们在巨地鸠没完没了相互指责的叫声中听到的焦躁不安。那些鸟儿抱怨找不到安宁，生气地说，难道不能安静下来吗？人们无法入睡，因为树上那些黑脑袋白身体的鸟儿整夜咕咕地叫着，诉说它们多么郁闷。它们说，听到老精灵在风中哭泣，心里充满巨大的悲伤。他们知道。他们应该已经感觉到有些东西一直在改变。那些人应该纳闷，为什么会发生这样的事情——古老的律法怎么会被打破？因为他们相信，自己一直非常严肃认真地继续老祖宗的事业，担当老祖宗交给的责任，让这里的故事经久不衰。因为在数不清的千年里，律法一直守护着这块魅力无穷的土地。

从林里，蕨类植物从大地的缝隙生长出来，古老的桉树被强风吹弯了腰。黎明前，鸟儿的歌声——品种太多，铃鸟、小鹦鹉、色彩斑斓的吸蜜鹦鹉——高亢嘹亮，悦耳动听，在空中回荡。黑暗中，合唱响起，宛若碧水涟漪先在广袤的丛林中飘忽，然后继续向内陆扩散。没多久，鸟儿的叫声就在整个大地鸣响，叽叽喳喳的声浪在天空下回荡。高高的桉树下面，灌木丛里，生活着蜥蜴、壁虎、蛇和别的小动物。黄毛野狗从鸟儿惊心动魄的叫声中嗅到非同寻常的事情正在发生。它们穿过灌木丛中的小路，钻进岩石间的秘密通道，跑回自己的洞穴，蜷缩成一团，闭上眼睛，一睡了之，全然不管洞穴外面的世界发生什么事情。

这一天，天还没亮，按照这一地区关于重要法律事务的故事，居住在海岬的达鲁（伊乌拉[03]）家族中最古老的卡迪迦尔[04]氏族，就被黑色雄性暴风鸟——噪鹃[05]受了惊吓的叫声吵醒。远处的噪鹃和它们遥相呼应。那和声与共鸣沿着“故事线”立刻传到几千公里之外的海岸，到达这块土地的另外一边。黑暗中，卡迪迦尔氏族的人们压低嗓门儿，用达鲁语轻声交谈。他们听出鸟儿啾啾啾的叫声中不无警告之意，但也知道这种叫声还有欢迎的意思。云开雾散，他们看到海湾里幽灵的白色，以为这是大海的祖先归来的景象，于是心气平和地互相说，鸟儿焦躁不安、大惊小怪的尖叫根本就没有必要。

他们刚刚停止谈论海上幽灵的事，就听到草原和沼泽传来褐翅鸦鹃[06]长时间的、咕咕咕的悲啼。没有人说这是什么不祥之兆，但这像祖先发出警告的故事。想明白这个故事的寓意，就会为下一步做什么、如何做指明方向。这个故事和新生婴儿有关吗？人们可能这样想。不过，这个念头在老人们心里一闪而过——也许还是以后再提这事儿为妙。他们开始和母亲、婴儿又说又笑。小宝贝刚出生几小时，躺在木头雕制成的库拉蒙里睡着，祖母抱着库拉蒙。之后，父亲把她举起来，介绍给她的祖先，让他们传统土地的所有创造者看。氏族的人们谈论如何给孩子取名字，才能够赋予他们特殊的使命和对土地的责任感，因为这是律法的要求。

女婴的名字已经取好，也得到老人们的首肯。因为那是一个和神圣的律法相关的名字，包蕴着古老的智慧。将她放在责任的网络中，就像别的无数的线条，遍布整个大陆，相互连接在一起。

清晨，袅袅炊烟从营地的篝火升起，在丛林弥漫开来。风中传来充满爱意的母亲们一遍遍呼唤、唠叨婴儿的名字的声音。这样老祖宗就能听到。这样就能为孩子创造记忆，让他们记住与世代相连的生命地图，确保婴儿听到的第一个声音，是她的民族的声音。晨曦初现，许多氏族成员聚集在海岬，眺望云雾缭绕的地平线，等待海风吹过，云开雾散。有的女人对着海水歌唱，讲述把大海造就成这个样子的祖先精灵的故事。也许她们在等待很快就会从这里经过的鲸鱼家族——按照律法，一直以来就是这样。再过一会儿，男人们就会走出来，欢迎鲸鱼，和它们谈论精神之旅，听鲸鱼的故事，就像和任何从门前经过的亲戚一样，畅诉心怀。

那天，薄雾散尽，氏族的人们才明白，属于他们的海景已经永远改变。鬼船停泊在那里，一个长长的故事就此展开。白鬼的数量越来越多。他们创造了战争，摧毁了这块土地古老的档案。千万年来，高级别的宗教守卫者把这些档案奉为神明，承担着众所周知的管理这块土地的责任。

芦苇的记忆

身体永远都会记着被追赶直到沉默无言的故事，记着逃跑永远不会再回来的故事；记着永远不会再回家，被奴役是什么感觉；记着炎炎烈日下被绑在树上，丢在那儿好几天的感觉；记着被鞭梢绑着铁刺的皮鞭抽得皮开肉绽、鲜血淋漓的感觉；记着被强奸的感觉；记着听到家人被杀害，哀求马背上的人不要抢走怀里的孩子，不要把孩子摔到岩石上，再扔到一边的感觉。不要杀死！还有你的土地被偷走，土地的故事被毁灭的感觉。档案中有哪些律法告诉你，如何阻止在自己的土地上，像害虫一样被迫害，被鄙视？当思想重启时，身体带着被追赶的记忆，走进未来几代人的梦想。

这些故事会不会讲述这个世界梦想着逃离，去寻找正在传统的陆地和海洋的故事中消失的守护者？我们的土地一定梦到这些守护者变成了什么样子。世界在它的阴影里做梦吗？对着失去灵魂的地方叹息？

很久以前，这块土地上的一位母亲听到白鬼占领了家园，就像世界历史上数百万饱受战争蹂躏的人们一样逃命。她是看到丈夫被一帮鬼子杀死之后逃亡的。她抱着孩子，茫无目的地跑过沼泽地，就像那些曾经跟着海神尼普顿在亚得里亚海的咸水沼泽中逃命的人一样，藏在威尼斯潟湖[08]的水道和浅滩之间的小岛上，像小鸟一样栖息在金合欢和柳树枝上。

和这个女人一起逃跑的氏族成员，也就是小宝宝的祖母和保护者，内心深处已经知道这个孩子的名字。这个多年来一直为他们的人民所喜爱的名字，将成为遥远的记忆，成为一个神圣地方的故事。这个女人知道自己已经变得什么都不是，因为她甚至感觉不到自己是谁，不知道自己在做什么。话语变得毫无用处，声音无法在她的嘴里形成。环顾四周，她被这个地方的故事吓坏了。她不应该在这个地方，远离她的梦想之地。她什么也听不见，甚至连小宝贝的哭声也听不见了。

她对这个世界充耳不闻，在被追逐的地方沉默不语。她一手抱着刚出生的小宝宝匍匐向前的时候，变成一个不可能存在的“无影存在”。她爬过绵延许多公里的低洼湿地的芦苇荡，沿着鸟和昆虫留下的踪迹、被野狗和巨蜥追赶的芦苇飞蛾的“航线”前进。夜晚，婴儿被母亲紧紧地抱着藏在潮湿的芦苇荡里，听到母亲那颗怦怦直跳的心的恐惧，感觉到母亲不停颤抖的身体，已经学会一声不吭。女人和家人一起藏在芦苇荡里的时候，不敢睡觉。她沉默着，仍然保持高度警惕，想说话的时候，只能打手势。当藏身的人倾听藏身的灌木丛时，大石鸻[09]变成精灵女人。感觉到危险的时候，身披灰色和棕色羽毛披风的精灵，就在水茫茫的芦苇丛中发出刺耳的哀鸣。凄婉的叫声在它们关于死亡的故事里回响，整个夜晚阴魂不散。黎明时分，枪声在薄雾中响起，一切都沉寂了。在这个没有鸟鸣的黎明，大地仿佛已经哀鸣了几百年。

燕子窝

她飞走了，那个女孩。某某某的女儿的女儿的女儿，等等，等等。从另一个地方来，遥远的地方，可怜的家伙，很久以前。从燕子筑巢的鬼屋逃了出来，又远道迁徙，飞回摇摇欲坠的墙壁，重建它们的泥巢。在准备开始漫长的迁徙之旅时，在一次紧张的飞行中，她的思绪掠过天空，就像鸟儿一边逃离俯冲而下的老鹰，一边追逐着昆虫。她也是为了活命才飞过来的。奔跑的时候，她对自己说什么来着？不喜欢黑人女仆的生活？难道她真的像人们说的那样，穿一件洁白的、镶漂亮花边的舞会礼服从房子的阴影里飞出来，只是因为迷失在辉煌梦想中耀眼的灯光里吗？那梦在她的思想里闪闪发光。

正是这样的愿景，穿过她心中像荆棘一样不断增长的不确定性。宛如无法穿透的灌木丛，矗立在眼前，阻挡她眺望地平线，告诉她做这，做那，似乎她从来没有做过一件正确的事。像我教给你的那样躺在床上。他们对她说，如果连床都不会收拾，不会弄得整洁完美，她就永远成不了气候。在她的想象中，用最微小的希望的工具劈砍出一条路，是一件荒诞不经的事。无穷无尽的夜晚的时光让草成熟变黄，她小心谨慎地拨开灌木丛，找到通往最奇妙的远方世界的路。那个世界隐藏在已播种的田野之外，直到遥远的地平线，却把她锁在偏远的农庄，被迫在那里工作。也许是繁星点点的天空挡住了一个年轻女人的梦想，她永远不知道厨房窗外是什么。她曾经站在那里好多年，久久地凝视着地平线。

一旦她飞走，这个地方历史上的悲哀就像垃圾一样不断地被扔向那个奇妙的世界。再远的距离也无法阻止她的思绪永远回到那个熟悉的地方，像燕子一样飞来飞去，体会那熟悉的悲凉。经过最漫长的旅行终于回来之后，她绕着那座快要坍塌的屋子走来走去，在白日梦里一遍又一遍抚摸墙壁。她常常在城市明亮的灯光下谈起那所古老的房子多么可爱，多么安静。仿佛站在遥远的地方，感受它的美好。她说，她在那里被善待。她在城市的灯光下和像燕子一样飞来飞去的男人跳舞。裙子像晾衣绳上挂着的衣服，在风中旋转。她看着燕子飞到排水沟，衔起污泥筑巢，保护快要坍塌的墙壁。

不一会儿，她就回到厨房窗前，用滚烫的热水洗碟子、盘子，然后又花了好长时间，慢悠悠地刷洗壶、盆、平底锅上的油污。她一边洗一边看灰色的尘土从风儿吹过的枯黄的草茬间升起。把她和她自己清晰的愿景联系到一起的内海从地平线漫延过来，越过平原，寻觅一个故事的记忆，寻找那个陷阱的蛛丝马迹。在那里，阴影其实就是身体本身[10]。

再次被地平线围困之后，她有时候觉得好像有一位似曾相识的姑娘就在身边。她是被驮在马背上送到这幢房子跟前的。正是这一形象，使她产生了一种永恒的感觉。那永恒之中，没有任何变化，唯一存在的叙述方式，是交织在一起可以互换的、混乱的记忆线。无私奉献的时候，她觉得自己是站在神圣之地的一个虔诚的信徒。在这里，她想象自己处于一种永久清洁的状态。她不停地寻找想象中田野里土壤的微粒，泥水绝不能溅到衣服上。衣服必须熨烫得平平整整，没有一个褶子，也不能有让人看出来自乡村的任何标志。她的窗户永远处于“清醒”的状态。这就要求她保持高度的警惕，防备未来可能发生的事情，等待往事重新出现在眼前，因为她心里埋藏着永远也解决不了的问题。

她将永远独自一人，被困在梦中那个阴暗的“档案馆”。尽管行走在城市拥挤的大街上，耳边回响着喧闹的市声，她还将继续被禁闭在寂静的鬼屋,眼看着它渐渐变成废墟。而燕子试图重建它的墙壁，以保存一个故事: 有一次看到一个小女孩儿被骑马的男人带到这里，没有亲人，没有同胞，变成了……

夜莺在哪里歌唱

这完全是一个谜，她已经走了——受够了这个地方，受够了这里的生活，受够了这里的一切。只有躯体留在这里。你能看到的只是一个在新时代、在世界另外一个地方凝望大海的女人的空壳。一位许多代逃亡者的后人。她的精灵，同一个古老的存在，想象中给你足够的力量继续向前，再多走一英里，可现在已经消失得无影无踪。精灵已经不在那儿了。它是许多年前从别的什么地方离开，快速从她的头脑中逃离。不停的战争吓坏了精灵，只能逃离一直逼她躲藏在大墙后面、生活在阴影中的暴力。可是后来，那个失去“乡土观念”的可怜的老精灵依然思乡心切，又悄悄地爬了回来。她知道自己别无选择，只能情意绵绵地依附那个女人，永远不能丢下她不管。在向不可能到达的地平线艰难跋涉的路上，她每迈出一步都变得更加艰难。但是自由精灵拉着她，脚步不停，一直向前。这条道路上，成千上万，不断增长的百万大军，曾经走过一千个昨天，走过跨越沙漠、踩过沙砾和泥土的旅程。然后，终于来到水边。站在通往最后的地平线、走进新生活的旅程下一个节点的时候，她的精灵在与众神的谈判中，怂恿、纵容了肮脏的人贩子，以寻求一条安全的通道穿越海洋。

努力吧，精灵。去和那些大人物谈谈。许多人压低嗓门儿的祈祷随风而去，飘过滚滚波涛。波涛下面住着早已被人们忘记的像大西洋波塞冬[11]这样的神。在这场想被神听到祈祷的竞赛中，有些人的呢喃细语甚至可能传到佛罗伦萨喷泉中凶猛的海神尼普顿和他的大理石海马那里。这些祈祷的人会加入世界各地码头上数百万祈祷者的行列。寻求跨越地中海的人可能向非洲海洋的女神叶玛亚[12]祈祷，或向阿格维祈祷；或者向海洋的统治者鲲龙祈祷。向从别的地方来的神祈祷，那里，海王的美人鱼女儿苏苏鲁[13]改变了海水。或者向萨蒙德拉[14]、维拉莫[15]、住吉三神[16]这样的神祈祷，他们推动着海浪和洋流。向海神和风暴之神须佐之男、绵津见神[17]、尼奥尔德[18]祈祷，或者向伐楼拿[19]——永恒海洋之主祈祷。向妈祖祈祷，她还在计算成千上万来寺庙烧香磕头的海上旅行者的人数。

在这个故事中，无数的人经历了人造沙漠的奴役，走到这一步。一路上，他们把生活中更多的东西交到危险的人手中，才终于到达一个被认为安全的地方。她站在吱吱嘎嘎作响的码头上等待的时候，思绪就像清晨的薄雾一样飘来飘去。这个码头看上去可能和世界上任何码头都一样。鱼腥味和大海的味道浓烈，瘦骨伶仃的猫抢食渔民祭献海神剩下的鱼骨头。挺立在黑暗中的烟囱上落着一只夜莺，正在唱悲凉的摇篮曲。偷渡的人和人贩子混在一起，偷偷地排着长队，准备乘坐根本不适合远航的船，驶往远方。

这只小夜莺唱着一首史诗般的旅行之歌。它可能是要迁徙数千英里到东南亚，或者为了补充物种而北上欧洲。也可能要回撒哈拉以南的非洲，那里是它过冬的故乡。这便是它的“蓝天之旅”。它仍然不停地歌唱，虽然天一亮便听不见它的歌声。女人一脸茫然，凝望着外面的港口，那里的船只和渔船几百年来一直行驶在这片安全的水域。她已经很久没有听过鸟儿歌唱了。鸟儿的歌声预示种庄稼的季节到了，也曾唤起她对早已被埋葬的男人夜里呼吸的记忆。可是现在，鸟儿的歌声对她来说已经没有意义。她梦见自己远离了传说中的乐土，走进另一个她用自己的生命塑造的传说。她将在自己的故事里沉入遗忘，成为乌有。

在这个码头上，毫无安全可言。她在风的吹拂下等待着，目无所视，紧紧抱在怀里的男婴，似乎已经感觉到他们即将分离。小东西看上去很不安，好像要切断和妈妈的联系。你可以看到他已经把她忘记，不停地挣扎，仿佛想要挣脱她的怀抱。

他的灵魂向凤尾蝶飞去。那是一只黑白相间、长着燕子尾巴的蝴蝶，生活在他的家乡。他看见它在他们身后飞翔——也许是来向远行的人们道别。一群沉默无语的人挤进等待着的渔船。这条船那么破旧，它曾经的主人一定是一位早已作古的水手。小男孩几乎要从紧紧抱着他的双臂中挣脱了，仿佛他是被一个渴望亲密带来温暖的陌生人抱着。他扭动着，挣扎着，想飞起来追随这只活在同胞们的传说中的蝴蝶，飞向黑暗的大街。世界各地成千上万的难民在那里争夺生存空间。它仿佛正领他回到他所知道的生活。在那里，飓风摧毁了棚户区，把破烂的渔船吹上天空。

小男孩已经像古老的风，从他住的包装箱的门溜了进来。包装箱是用钉子钉在一起，又用绳子和铁丝捆扎塑料和铁皮建造而成的“家”。这是母亲从难民遗弃的一大片破烂窝棚中找到的。她在这里独自生下在路上被士兵强奸而怀上的孩子。成千上万人的喧闹声摇晃着他的摇篮。这些人在拥挤不堪、充满威胁和被控制的狭小空间里生活。这就是家的感觉，他的家人，哄他入睡的声音。也许她知道，大海的涛声惊扰了婴儿。一位神已经对他说话。她独自一人走了，在大海的庇护下，感受着渔船和帆船的运动。这些船远离沙漠，开始几千英里的航行。沙漠里，成千上万的人像动物一样踏上逃亡之路。

那些男人笼罩在香烟的烟雾中，拿人们的命运做交易时表现得镇定自若。几个月来，他们一直告诉她，如果她能相机行事，善于应变，他们很愿意向她这样的女人提供帮助。他们说她的故事已经预先编好。他们说，她是拿命运做赌注。其实，直到最后付清他们的要价，她也只抓住了一半的机会。大雾迷蒙，几条渔船停泊在码头下面。阴霾笼罩的码头，只有一盏路灯发出枯黄的光。她现在属于一个偏执狂的世界，人们在一片混乱中拼命往船上挤。她惊慌失措，心里明白，虽然还有那么多人争抢着要上船，实际上那里已经没有立锥之地。

她凝视着那几百张脸，人们紧紧地挤在一起，从拥挤不堪、早已超载的船上盯着她看。非常危险，但她知道别无选择，只能在还有一线希望的时候，拼命向前挤。钱花光了，再也付不起了。快点！快点！赶快上船，你这个笨蛋！没有时间了，她感觉到汹涌的人群中有人把她向小船推去。匆忙之中，她设法一条胳膊抱住她那个小包袱，另一条胳膊紧紧搂住孩子。盯着她看的人和那些还在拼命往船上挤的人脸上都露出绝望的表情。这表情让她意识到，这个地方古老的神正在摇晃这条船。

那么多人挤在船上，挤得越来越紧，站立不稳。她已经意识到，人们之所以吓得发出无声的尖叫，是因为已经预见到海神早已遗忘了他们。她出于本能想逃走。挤在船上的乘客故意让船摇晃，不让她上去。拥挤的船已经不堪重负，她心如明镜。此时此刻，她清清楚楚地看到，无数只手像海浪一样从船上扑来，想把她和孩子在她试图登船的一霎，从码头上推下去。他们将落入已经变成墨黑的大海。

在这千钧一发、命运攸关的时刻，万籁俱寂，只有海水拍打船身的声音和远处雾角号与船钟在起伏的海浪上摇晃时发出的响声。那个坏警察使劲往船上推她——他的记录还算干净，只是像旅行社里供着的海神一样收取些费用，并且决心在不被发现的情况下把最后一批货物运上船。即使大家都在注视他作为一个警察已经超越自己的“辖区”也不在乎。这当儿，那么多只手都伸出来，不让她上船。她不得不按照瞬间闪现的想法为今后的人生之路做出抉择。平常她听人家说的那些话在耳边响起：像她这样通过不正当渠道出海的人都会受到不公平的待遇。她看到码头下，死去的人被根本就不知道他们是何许人也的神漫不经心地摇晃着。然后，一连串无尽的银色人脸肖像从她眼前掠过，这是那些从地球的其他地方试图横渡大海是死去的人。她看见他们和她自己一样，背负着永恒的重负沉没下去，永远无法抵达目的地。

倏忽之间，她第一次真正把事情想透，仿佛看见自己和孩子掉进大海，加入到其他“多余的货物”之中。或者像世界某一个地方冥神幽暗缠绕的海草森林里的死人一样，或者就葬身在码头下面，葬身在广阔的繁藻地轻轻摇曳的波西多尼亚海草[20]之中。船身已经被海水淹没一半，甲板上的人站立不稳，就像摇篮里的婴儿晃来晃去，十分危险。危难时刻，一切都不容多想。警察最后一把，把她推上甲板。就在她踉踉跄跄站起身来的一瞬，她突然想到，日后，她没有什么办法去教育孩子，连忙把孩子交给警察。警察已经把船推离码头，然后朝船身踢了一脚。船驶进夜色笼罩的大海。

守灵夜

人们说，一条破旧的渔船满载几百名乘客，在大海遇到风暴失去控制。渔船开始倾斜的时候，人们一个压着一个乱作一团。他们试图用手指抓住海浪中颠簸的破船的船身，但是狂暴的大海波涛汹涌，人们互相冲撞着，谁都坚持不住。等到渔船完全翻过来，吓坏了的人们都被抛进大海。海浪拍打着陡峭的岩石海岸，落水的人像海浪中的海草，漂来漂去。许多人被淹死。也许像她之前的许多人和成千上万的后来人一样，女人还有最后一次机会呼喊她留在岸上的孩子的名字。也许当她沉入无边海草中的水底坟墓时，她意识到，她已经教给孩子如何活下去。

他们叫什么名字？他们是谁？你一定好奇。所有这些人的名字是什么？在史诗般的故事中，千百年来他们曾经是自己家园的守护者，就像那土地曾经是他们的守护者一样。

用带刺的铁丝网、钢板、砖块、石头、钢筋水泥砌成的墙，以及我们为防止他人进入而在心里建造的监狱，这些都需要我们时刻保持警惕。他们不能来这里。像神一样，我们变成了一支守望者的军队，焦虑地保卫着自己，不受陌生人世界的侵扰。特权阶层从自建的瞭望塔里满腹狐疑地凝望外面的世界，想避开一个事实：今天，世界上有六千五百三十万流离失所的人，他们只有一个简单的梦想——活下去。我们说，他们不在我们的掌控之下。世界人口一百一十三分之一的人是难民。几百万人在逃命，几百万人几十年来一直困在外国的难民营里。对于那些正在遭受迫害的人，那些正在这个星球上四处游荡、寻找避风港和栖身之所的人，那些试图重新开始生活的人，那些梦想着回家的人，生死攸关的时刻已经到来。

她叫什么名字——那个抱着男孩的女人。他叫什么名字？世界上那些无家可归的人，数百万需要新时代曙光的人的名字是什么？我们知道这些人的家庭、氏族、部落给他们起的是什么名字吗？他们给孩子起的名字都有特别的含义。那名字是对未来的祝福吗？就像1788年植物湾海岬地区那个女婴被赐予一个可爱的名字一样。或者像那个命运多舛的母亲把亲生的婴儿交给人贩子时，稍加思索，做出决定的名字。这几百万人是不是都有一个多少世纪以来人们熟知的名字，一个意味着巨大快乐的名字？或者沿用守护自己氏族的人的名字，或者表示值得信赖的名字——做一个让人放心又有价值的人。或者用晨光命名，表示希望。希望孩子当教师，做一个勇敢无畏的人，做一个想象力丰富的人。或者以亲爱的故乡命名，那里有最甜的蜜枣和最美的鲜花。或者以高山、沙漠里重要的花朵命名。或者以天神之子命名，充满希望，亲切温柔，成为神的仆人、部落的中坚，博学、聪明，给人以启迪，一个充满同情心的仆人。或者一个受人崇拜的人，人民、朋友都爱戴他。或者以一只鹿、一头羚羊命名。或者以家乡一片风景宜人的橄榄树林命名。或者那名字表示原谅、慷慨、光耀千秋，或者以这个国家最古老的寓言中一个值得尊敬的人物命名，或者以一位受人爱戴的女神命名，或者，她是以一个值得称赞的人命名?

注

01 不列颠尼亚（Britannia）：罗马帝国对不列颠岛的古意大利语称呼，后据此设立不列颠尼亚行省。

02 布兰（Brân the Blessed）：威尔士神话中英国的一位巨人国王。布兰这个名字在威尔士语中通常翻译为乌鸦。

03 伊乌拉（Eora）：澳大利亚的土著居民。他们的传统领地从南部的乔治河和植物湾延伸到杰克逊港，北部到霍克斯伯里河河口的比特沃特，西部沿河到帕拉马塔。土著人自认是 Eora，字面意思是“人民”，这个词来源于 Ee（是的）和 ora（这里，或者这个地方）。他们的语言也被称为 Eora。伊乌拉人有着跨越数千年的传统遗产。

04 卡迪迦尔（Cadigal）：也被拼写为 Gadigal，澳大利亚土著居民，他们最初居住在他们称为“Cadi”的地区。位于杰克逊港以南，覆盖了今天的悉尼 CBD。卡迪迦尔语言是达鲁语言的派生。总督亚瑟·菲利普抵达杰克逊港后不久，估计悉尼地区的土著居民大约有 1500 人，不过其他估计数字从 200 人到 4000 人不等。

05 噪鹃（Koel Cuckoo）：噪鹃是热带的一种布谷鸟，它潜伏在灌木丛中，发出有节奏的似狼的叫声。

06 褐翅鸦鹃（Coucal）：俗名大毛鸡、毛鸡、红毛鸡。

07 库拉蒙（Coolamon）：澳大利亚原住民用木头或树皮制作的浅盘，放水果和别的东西。

08 威尼斯潟湖（Venetian Lagoon）：亚得里亚海的一个封闭海湾，威尼斯市就坐落在这里。

09 大石鸻：学名 Esacus magnirostris，主要栖息于澳大利亚的海滨沙滩、岩礁和海边红树林地区。

10 作者注：where the shadows are really the body，引自伊丽莎白·毕肖普的诗《失眠》。

注

11　波塞冬（Poseidon）：古希腊神话中的海神，奥林匹斯十二主神之一。

12　叶玛亚（Yemaya）：约鲁巴神话里的海洋之神，是孩子们的坚强保护者。

13　阿格维（Agwe）：海地伏都教的海神，统治海洋、鱼类和水生植物的神，同时也是渔民和水手的保护神。

14　维拉莫 (Vellamo)：芬兰神话中水、湖和海的女神。据说她又高又漂亮，深受渔民们的尊敬，他们向她祈祷捕鱼好运。

15　住吉三神（Sumiyoshi Sanjin）：日本神话中的海神和航海家。

16　绵津见神（Watatsumi）：传说中的日本龙和守护水神。

17　尼奥尔德（Njord）：挪威神话中的海洋之神。

18　伐楼拿（Varuna）：印度教中的天神，是掌管法律、秩序的神祇。

19　波西多尼亚（Posidonia oceanica）：也称大海洋神草，寿命超过 10 万年的无性繁殖海草。

Odyssey of the Horizon

Alexis Wright

THE OLD WIND

The waves you see will continue to heave and wash away boundaries of imagined borders, and mighty storms of the times will erode and break down the walls we build in our minds to imprison ourselves, just as the barricades erected with steel and barbwire to keep other people out will be broken. There are no boundaries in the ocean's currents stirring the waters we have touched for the fish to feel, and nothing that will stop any forgotten God living under the waves from weighing up what our will is worth. We breathe air mingled with the breath of others, and even the old wind that blows around the place always creates its rattle-and-skittle symphony from our trash for all to hear.

On the horizon one day, at Weé-rong or Warran (Sydney Cove), in the language of the southern continent's Darug (Eora) nation belonging to this part of the land, white ghosts arrived to break the boundary of a land that was not theirs to take. The old wind spirit guarding the coastline slipped through the nooks and cracks of the ghost ships, smelt its stench of death, and felt the fear of the white ghosts while pressing her cheek against the slimy sides of the vessels, and against the grimy pallid skin of its prisoners. The terribleness she sensed was manifest and foretold. She recoiled, fled from the fear like a stricken animal. Then, like some old aunty, she stormed off over the waves while screaming in rage, and leaving trails of spit in her wake. She sped wildly away, up and down the coast, and dragged clouds of migrating butterflies with her in gusts of wind howling over the sea while she tried to clean her pristine skin.

Up in the atmosphere, she sped thousands of kilometres around the continent to spread the news of her violation, and then the most major ancestral spirit started bringing up the northern cyclones and gale-force winds to rip down the eastern coastline, and it stirred the skies across the country with black storm clouds in its dance of thunder and lightning, while the mighty ancestors living under the waves, rattling and shaking the strange floating ghost ships rocking on the crest of waves, could not make them go away. The ships remained silent, like some dead things that was devoid of spirit. The timber hulls gave up nothing of their essence to the ancestral creation beings who had made this place. There was not a word of communication about their trespass, and nothing else was heard by the ancestors except for the *ding, dong, ding* of ship bells, and unknown voices – not Gods – shouting demands.

This had been an epical eight-month sea journey for the initial eleven ghost ships of the invasion that had set sail from a faraway Britannia, from where ancestor Gods like Brân the Blessed, the old king God called a crow, had taught men how to rule by the sword. A brutal, conquering kind of people moved about on the ships with bloodstained whips, guns and the enslaving ways of their old war Gods flowing strong in the bloodstream, and down in the cargo hold, the sea of Manannán mac Lir, son of a sea God, also flowed through the veins of many of its prisoners.

On board the wooden ships with their great flowing canvas sails, a flurry in the wind, there were one thousand, three hundred and thirty-six living souls on 26 January, more than two centuries ago, in 1788. Most were convicts kept in the overcrowded holds of some of the ships. Just a lot of poor souls convicted of some crime, mostly petty and insignificant, hardly warranting a punishment of being sent far away from their homeland to the other side of the world forever, to be forced by the whip to labour in a plan to establish a penal colony. Their faraway government, and the government that was established on this continent in the name of a British Queen, just believed then, and went on believing that this country was uninhabited, because its inhabitants – *Well! Blacks* – were less than human.

It would take two centuries for those who followed the initial trespassers to recognise through the High Court of Australia that the traditional owners who occupied the entire continent had one of the most highly developed and sophisticated ancient law and governance systems in the world that cared for the country in its entirety – as holy places, the whole country forming the biggest law cathedral on earth. This was a library land, its knowledge stored in and created from the country itself through epical stories from ancient times. An almost unimaginable massive archive, cared for by its people through their spiritual connections to various parts of the physical landscape.

The epical stories were the continent's foundation laws, kept sacred for countless millennia, and had been continuously renewed and read in ceremonies by the caretakers of their story country. These librarians of high religious order had kept this knowledge alive since, their dependents would still say, the beginning of time. But sadly for the traditional owners, this invasion never stopped, and all of its dire consequences continue to this day.

Imagine on the day the white ghost ships arrived, how totally shocked the Darug people would have been to see hundreds of people looking like ghosts leave these ships, disembarking on the sands of this country, with no connection or interest in the powerful of the traditional law stories of this place. It must have been a total shock to see what, in terms of today's world population, would have looked like eleven thousand strangers turning up, and the Darug people would have known that the ignorance of the white ghosts would make the spirits of the country dangerous.

OF BELONGING TO COUNTRY

Imagine the ships arriving, and what the traditional owners of the country would have known of the oldest law stories governing their land, from that immense body of knowledge in their law book for belonging that was held in the mind and read from the country itself. A guide created and given by the ancestors, preserved and continuously passed down the generations in the longest surviving culture in the world. How noticeable any change would have been to a people immersed in so much ancient knowledge of looking after country, where even the most minuscule change such as the movement in waters could be detected, and deciphered.

Would these people, in this first contact with the white ghost people, have gathered together in a huddle of bullies hell-bent on out-bullying each other in order to form an operation sovereign border policy, and prepared for war with the invaders by carving a million spears for a million warriors, or built a stone wall around the entire country to imprison themselves by keeping everybody else out? Or else created off-shore detention camps in a poor neighbouring country for locking up these boat people for the rest of their natural lives? No. The ancestral stories would have guided them differently, their logic and thinking would have been based on the law stories that had always led them, to do what their most important ancestors would have done – perhaps sought knowledge, reciprocal understanding to uphold their ancient laws, to keep the country alive, to keep it from becoming dangerous.

These ancestors had highly sophisticated practices that tied them to their storylines for this part of the country, where they were guided by its laws. Those old people, who came from a long line of men and women well versed in the practice of laws for caring for this country, would have noticed the story of the dance of the sea, or known the mood of breezes or a butterfly's flight, or how to read the ancestral stories to the battering gales of storms, or of wind gusts lashing hard rain, or when rain refused to fall at all. They would have known how to see the ocean as it had always been seen in its ways and habits, and would have spoken to it often in long song cycles they regularly performed, and read the signs in known stories that had been passed down to them through countless millennia.

Let us say then, the howling sea was being read by the traditional owners of this part of the country, maybe who knows from several days previously, or even months before the ships with white sails arrived. *Old woman must be crying, what for*, they might have said about this. They would have known how the sea breezes should be moving for this time of year because they were closely related to the ancestor, but instead, the relative held so dear and beloved had been disturbed, and begun to behave strangely. They had known nothing like this before, even as the blustery winds hit the weathered sandstone escarpment, and you could hear the whispering heard by some important families for country who were now camping and waiting for the unexpected, perhaps waiting with the ancestors rising from the country that had already seen white ghosts in the atmosphere overlooking the sea.

They may already have felt the invasion's enormity in their bones, felt that some important essence of life was being tugged out of their bodies by an unusually strange occurrence – the fast-paced continuous cooing of troubled wonga pigeons – and then, of feeling they were becoming shadow people, and in this feeling of great vulnerability, felt what it was like to be searching an endless future to find again the essence of one's soul. The old men and women kept talking to the country's spirits in hushed voices, trying to calm a restlessness they could hear in the endless chatter of the pigeon birds annoying one another, that could find no peace and would not be quietened. These people hardly slept now thanks to the noise of these black-head and white-body spirit birds far up in the trees coo-cooing all night, saying how troubled they felt. They talked of being overcome with such enormity of sadness, flooding them as they heard these old spirits crying in the wind. *They knew*. They would already have sensed something was changing for all times, and those people may have wondered how this could have happened – how the old laws had been broken – because they believed they had continued to carry out the responsibilities of their ancestors very seriously, and had kept the stories strong and alive for the laws that had looked after this powerful place for untold millennia.

From a place where ferns grew out of the crevices, in the bushland of old eucalypts bent by strong winds, the songs of birds too numerous in varieties – bellbirds, cockatoos, lorikeets –of multicolours and canorous sounds, were filling the country with an extra-heightened crescendo of song well before dawn. In the darkness, a chorus rippled, and began to be repeated through vast stretches of bushland and continued further inland, so that before too long, the cries of birds were being repeated and returned in waves of chatter, across the entire country. In the thickets below the tall gum trees, where the lizards, geckos, snakes and other animals lived, yellow-coated dingos sensed the uncertainty in the alarming bird cries, and were already cantering away through their lanes in the undergrowth, sauntering into secret hideaways among the rocks, rolling themselves in tight balls inside caves of sacredness, and closing their eyes to sleep away what was happening in the world outside their dens.

Even before dawn, these oldest Gadigal clanspeople from families of the Darug people, on the headlands for important law business about the stories of this area, were awakened by the startled cries of the black male storm bird, the koel cuckoo, and then felt its call reverberating through other koels further away, where the echoes instantaneously carried its storyline right around the coast of many thousands of kilometres to reach the other side of the country. The clans recognised the bird's *quoy, quoy, quoy* warning call but knew it could also have been a greeting, while they were talking in low voices, almost whispering in the darkness to each other in the Darug language. They watched the fog lift, then saw the whiteness of ghosts out in the bay, and perhaps thought the phenomenon was ancestors of the sea returning, and they were quietly saying to each other that the birds' adagio seemed unnecessarily agitated.

Then no sooner had they stopped speaking to each other about the sea ghosts, than the long, repetitious coop-coop moaning call of the swamp coucal could be heard coming from the grasslands and swamps. Nobody said anything about the premonition, but it was like a story of ancestors calling a warning to think of its story, which would give them direction about what to do. Was this something to do with the new baby (this was what might have been thought), and it crossed the old peoples' mind to leave it alone right then – perhaps they would speak of it later. They began talking and laughing now with the mothers and babies, the newest member, born only hours before, sleeping in a wooden carved coolamon nestled in her grandmother's arms after her father had held her up and introduced his child to her ancestors – for all the creators of their traditional lands to see. And these clanspeople spoke together about how the names given to their children will always have a special meaning, with responsibilities for country, because this was the law.

This baby girl's name was already known and had been agreed upon by the old people, because it was a loved name associated with laws that had been kept sacred, and that carried ancient wisdom and meaning, and because of this would place her in a web of responsibilities and links, like countless other lines running throughout the entire continent and connecting it together.

In these early hours of the morning, as smoke rose from camp fires and spread through the bush, you could hear in the wind mothers calling and cooing the baby's name over and over so the ancestors would hear it, and so, by creating memories for the child of a life map linked to the ages, making sure that the first sounds the baby knew were the voices of her people. Many of the clan gathered on the heads as the morning light set in were looking out onto the horizon covered fog, waiting for the wind to pick up. Some women were singing to the water, telling the story of the ancestral spirits that charged the waters and had made it so. And maybe they were waiting for the family of whales soon to be passing, just as they had always done according to the law; later on, the men would go out and greet the whales, to talk to them about their spirit journeys, and listen to the whales' stories, as they would to any other relatives coming by.

When the mist lifted on that day the clanspeople knew the seascape had changed forever. The ghost ships stayed, and so began a long story about how these ghosts kept increasing in numbers, and creating wars to destroy much of the land's ancient archives, kept sacred for scores of millennia by the guardians of high religious degree who had the storied responsibilities of caring for this country.

THE MEMORY OF REEDS

A body always remembers the stories of the chase into silence, of escaping and never going back, of never reaching home again, of what it feels like to be enslaved, of how it feels being tied to a tree in the hot sun and left there for days, and to be beaten with a whip with barbwire attached to the end of its strands until every part of your skin has been cut into ribbons, or of being raped, and what it felt like hearing your family being murdered, begging for your children not to be dragged from your arms by men on horseback and then swung against a rock and tossed aside, *do not kill*, and of your lands stolen and its stories destroyed. What laws were in the archives that told you how to stop being persecuted and despised like vermin on your own land? While the mind begins afresh, the body carries the memories of the chase far into the dreams of the generations to come.

Would the stories say that the world should dream itself into escaping, of searching for its caretakers who were missing from the stories of their traditional land and seas? Country must dream of what becomes of these caretakers. Does the world dream in its shadow? Sigh at lost spirit places?

A long-ago traditional mother of this country who heard the white ghosts taking over the land would have run for her life like many millions of other war-torn people in the history of the world. She ran after seeing her husband killed by a pack of ghost men. She carried her baby away, as she ran blindly through the swamp lands to escape, just like those frightened people, running for their lives, had once followed their Neptune sea God among the salty marshes of the Adriatic Sea, and hidden in the small islands amongst the channels and shoals of a Venetian lagoon, where they lived like birds on platforms of wattle and the shoots of the willow tree.

The members of the clan who ran with the woman, the grannies and protector of the baby, already knew deep in their hearts that the child's name, which had been loved by their people through the ages, would become a distant memory of a sacred place story. The woman knew she had become nothing because she could not even feel what she was any more. She did not even know what she was doing. Words became nothing. Sound unable to form in her mouth as she looked all around herself, and was frightened by the story of this part of the country where she should not be, away from her Dreaming place. She could hear nothing any more, not even the cries of her baby.

Deaf to the world, and silenced where she was being chased, she became a non-existent shadowless presence as she crawled on her belly with the tiny newborn baby in one arm. She moved through the reeds covering many kilometres of low-lying wetlands. She followed the tracks of birds and insects, the flight of reed moths that had been chased by dingos and goannas. The baby had already learnt about silence by listening to the fear of her mother's thumping heart, a trembling body, while being held close in the watery reed tickets at night. But this woman dared not sleep while hiding with her family. Silenced, she remained alert, speaking only in hand signals, as the hidden listened to the hidden bush stone-curlews becoming spirit women. Sensing danger, the spirits of grey and brown feathered cloaks sent their high-pitched wails across the watery expanse of reeds. The night became haunted with their calls echoing back and forth in their tales about death, then were silenced when rifle shots rang in the mist at dawn. In this dawn without bird call, it felt as though the land had started to mourn for hundreds of years.

THE SWALLOWS' HOUSE

She flew off. That girl. Daughter's daughter's daughter of so and so's, so forth and so on from some other place, long way off, poor thing, one time ago. Escaped from the spirit house where swallows nest and return to its crumbling walls from flights of migration to rebuild their mud nests. In a nervous flight, her thinking flitted in the skies like these birds, chasing insects while rushing away from plunging eagles, in the time of becoming ready for the moment to fly off on their long migration. She had flown for her life too. What did she tell herself as she ran – that she did not like the black maid's life? Did she literally fly from the shadows of the house in a pure white ball gown of fine lace like people say, just to lose herself in the incautious bright lights of a splendid dream that gushed with splendour in her mind?

It was visions like this that could push their way right through the uncertainty that grew in her mind like brambles, an impenetrable thicket constructed to block her view of the horizon by voices telling her to do this and do that, that she never did anything right, *lie in the bed like I showed you*, that told her that she would never become anything because the bed could never be put back tidily in shape and perfect enough. It was monstrous to hack a track with the tiniest tool of hope in her imagination. Stem by stem, she parted the thickets and, through endless night-time mellow yellow grasses, found her way to a most wondrous faraway world that lay hidden beyond the isolation of sown fields to every horizon, and that had locked her in a remote homestead where she had been forced to work. Maybe it was just too many starry skies that got in the way of a young woman's dreams of never knowing what lay outside the kitchen window from where she had once stood for years and stared for so long at the horizon.

Then once she had flown, the history sadness of this place was continuously thrown around like trash at the wondrous world. No distance would ever be far enough to stop her thoughts from forever returning to a sense of knowing this one place, of migrating to and fro like a swallow, to this familiar sorrow. She walks slowly around the crumbling house, takes her time while touching its walls over and over again in her daydreams, after travelling the longest distances to get back. She frequently talked in the bright lights of the city about how lovely and quiet that old house was, and as though she was standing far away in the remoteness, feeling how good it felt, where she was always well treated, she said. She dances in city nights with men that are like swallows that flit to and fro while her dress swirls like clothes billowing in the wind on the clothes line of that place, where she watches the swallows fly to the drain to collect droplets of mud to construct their nest to preserve the walls.

It only takes moments to be back at the kitchen window to wash the dishes in scalding hot water, then leisurely spend ages cleaning grease from pots and pans while looking at the grey dust rise over the windswept yellow-grass-stubbled landscape, her inland sea, which linked her to a clear vision of herself travelling back from the horizon, over the flat plains, in search of the memories of a story, to find the little bits and pieces of the entrapment, *where the shadows are really the body.**

While being entrapped again by this horizon, she sometimes felt as though there was a young girl whom she might have once known, who was being carried to the house on horseback. It is this image that fed into her sense of a timelessness where nothing changes, where the only narratives that exist were interchangeable jumbled-up threads of memories, and in her devotion, it felt as though she was a deeply religious person in a place of worship. This was where she kept her imagined self in a perpetual state of cleanliness, where she was constantly searching for grains of soil of country, the mud that must never splash on her clothes, which should always be properly ironed and without any creases, nor be marked with a sense of country in any way. Her window belonged to an eternal state of wakefulness that required a heightened sense of vigilance, to be on guard against the future, to wait for the past to show up, for what could never be resolved in her mind.

* 'Insomnia', a poem by Elizabeth Bishop, poemhunter.com.

She would always be alone, caught in a shadowy archive of what was already dreamt even as she walked crowded city streets, and in the loud jazz of life she will remain trapped in the silent spirit house, and watching it crumbling into ruins while swallows try to rebuild its walls to conserve a story of once seeing a little girl brought in on the men's horses without her people, and becoming...

WHERE A NIGHTINGALE SINGS

This was the complete enigma of the thing, she was already gone – had it up to the eyeballs with this place, with life, the lot. Only the body remained. An empty shell was all that you saw left of the woman staring out to sea in a new time, in another part of the world, a descendant of too many generations left on the run. Her spirit, that same old thing that was supposed to give you enough sustenance to keep going, to take that extra mile, had disappeared. It was not there. Somewhere else long ago, the thing had left, sped from her head, itself frightened from wars that never stop, escaped the violence that kept her hiding behind walls, to live in shadows. But the thing was, this poor old homesick spirit that had lost its sense of country came crawling back. It knew it had no choice but to remain in a way sentimentally attached to the woman, and could never leave her alone. In its odyssey of making every step she took just that bit harder in her journeys towards reaching the unreachable horizon, the loose spirit kept dragging her on roads that had put tens of thousands, many growing millions, on a thousand yesterdays' road trip over desert sands, gravel and clay soils. Then finally at the water's edge, when she stood on the next point of the journey towards the final horizon to reach a new life, it was the spirit that egged and connived in its negotiations with the Gods and sleazy people-traffickers for a safe passage to cross the ocean.

Go for it, spirit. Talk it up to the big ones. Many whispered prayers flew off in the wind blowing across the waves where old forgotten Gods like Poseidon of the Atlantic lived. In the race to be heard, some of those prayers might even have reached a fierce Neptune standing with his marble seahorses in a Florence fountain. These prayers would have joined those of the millions that have prayed on the wharfs of the world. Those seeking their crossing of the Mediterranean sea who might have prayed to Yemaya, the African Goddess of the living ocean, or Agwe, or Yu-Kiang ruler of the ocean, or from elsewhere, where Susulu the mermaid daughter of the sea king shifted the waters, or Gods moving the waves and sea currents like Samudra, Vellamo, Sumiyoshi sanjin or Susanoo, God of storms and the sea, Watatsumi, Njord, or Varuna – Lord of the Eternal Ocean – or Mazu, who was still counting the millions of prayers and incense sticks burnt in temples from travellers of the seas.

In a story that had taken countless numbers of people through an enslavement of man-made deserts to reach this point and along the way, by placing more of life into the hands of dangerous people, to come somewhere that was supposed to be safe. Her mind was drifting like the mist in that early dawn as she waited on a creaking wharf that might have looked like any other in the world. Places where the smell of fish and the sea was strong, and where all the bony pussy cats scraped to catch fish bones flung by fishing men to sea Gods, or where a nightingale sang its mournful lullaby from a chimney stack in the darkness, while people queued secretly with the people-smugglers to board some unseaworthy boat that would take them away.

The little nightingale sang an epical song of journeys, which might either have been about migrating thousands of miles to South-East Asia, or Europe to replenish its species, or of the journey for blue skies in migration to its wintering homeland, back in sub-Saharan Africa. Yet it continued singing nonstop and unheard in rising light, even as the woman stared blankly out onto the harbour, where ships and fishing boats had been using these safe waters for centuries. It had been a long time since she had listened to bird song that once signified seasons for crops or planting, or a memory of her buried man's breath in the night. A bird's song had no meaning for her any more. She was far away in her dream of being elsewhere from fabled places, to be in another fable she was fashioning with her life, in her story of sinking into oblivion, of never existing.

There was no safety in this wharf for her as she waited with the wind at play, to stare at nothing. The baby boy she held tightly to her had already sensed their future separating. He looked restless, as though he was cutting himself loose from her, and you could see that he was already forgetting her as he kept pulling away, as though he wanted to fly from her arms.

His spirit was charging towards the *papilio*, a black and white swallowtail butterfly of his homeland that he watched flying behind them – perhaps coming to say goodbye to its people leaving, a multiple of silent human souls starting to fill up the waiting fishing boat – a vessel so old that an ancient mariner might have once owned it. The baby boy almost recoiled from the arms holding him tightly, as though he was being held by a stranger craving the warmth of his closeness. He squirmed and strained, wiggling to fly after the butterfly of his peoples' legends, heading into the darkened streets where tens of thousands of the world's displaced people jostled for living space, as though it was leading him back towards what he knew of life, a place where cyclones ripped these shanty towns apart and sent rotten fishing boats flying into makeshift life.

Baby boy was already like the old wind that slipped through the door of his dwelling of packing cases nailed together, plastic and sheet iron tied with bits of rope and wire. The abandoned place of a long line of refugees that his mother had found in which to give birth alone to a child conceived by rape on the road by soldiers. The cradle he knew was rocked by the noise of thousands of people living cheek by jowl in tight, overcrowded, threatened and controlled space. This was what felt like home, his family, the sounds that lulled him to sleep. Perhaps she knew this too, that the sound of the sea disturbed the baby. A God had already spoken to him. She was already travelling alone, sheltered by the sea, feeling the movement of fishing boats and ships travelling thousands of miles away from deserts where tens of thousands herded like animals on the run.

The men concealed in their cigarette haze, acted calming while making deals with peoples' lives. They had been telling her for months how they wanted to help women like her if she played her cards right. Her story they said, was foretold. Gamble fate, they said, until finally, having paid their price, she was half embarking on her only chance, some broken-down fishing boat docked in the fog, tied up below the wharf. In the dim haze of the wharf's only street light, she now belonged to a world of paranoia, with everyone boarding the boat chaotically, and she was already panicking, because she knew in her heart that there would not be enough room for any more people still struggling to get on board.

She stared at the faces of hundreds of people standing, and huddled together, who stared up at her from the overcrowded boat. Nothing felt safe, but she knew there was nothing else to do but go while she had the chance. Her money was spent, and she could pay no more. Hurry! Hurry! Get on board, you fool! There could be no other time for her, and she felt someone from among those surging to get on board pushing her towards the boat. She tried in those rushed moments to manage the bundle of her belongings in one arm and the baby held tighter in the other, and perhaps she already sensed in the desperation on the faces staring at her and others that still needed to get on board, that it must be the ancient God of this place who was rocking the boat.

With so many people now crammed on board they all stood unsteadily while being pushed tighter together, and the realisation came to her like a silent scream of fear from all these people who were already foreseeing the sea journey over a sea God who did not remember them. She sensed already, in her instinct to flee, that the other passengers cramming together were deliberately swaying, rocking the boat, trying to make it impossible for her to go aboard. The boat was now crammed. She knew this in her guts, and she knew right there and then that the sea of hands reaching out to her from the boat, would push her and the baby off the side of the wharf as she tried to board, and they would fall into the now ink-blackened sea.

Perhaps it was in these fast panicked moments of a hushed decision of fate, where nothing was heard except water lapping the sides of boats, and the distant sound of foghorns and ships' bells rocking in the swells, as she was being roughly pushed to board by the corrupt cop – his record clean – who had collected the fares like some travel-agent ocean God, and was determined to get the last of his cargo on board undetected even as if anyone was watching his beat, and while the hands of so many reached out to stop her from boarding, that she was forced to navigate the rest of her life in a few split seconds of flashing thoughts of those rumours she had heard in common talk floating around about people getting a rough deal on some shonky passage like this, and in her mind, she saw dead people underneath the wharf being rocked carelessly by a God who had no clue who these people were. And then, quick silver images parade endless faces of strangers who had died far out at sea in a crossing from anywhere else on the planet. They were as she sees herself sinking with the weight of eternity and never reaching her destination.

It was over in just an instant – the first time she really thought it through, of watching herself and the baby falling into the sea to join other excess cargo, like the dead among a ghost God's tangled kelp forest in one part of the world, or in another, Posidonia oceanica, the vast seaweed bed swaying down below the wharf. The sea of people standing unsteadily on the half-submerged hull keep rocking it about like a baby's cradle. It sways precariously, and almost without thought in a life-or-death decision, in the final shove forward, where to steady her fall in that split second of thinking she had nothing to reach for to teach her child, she handed the baby to the policeman already shoving the boat off from the wharf and into the watery darkness with his boot.

THE VIGIL

They say that hundreds of people were on board an old and broken-down fishing boat that had started to list uncontrollably at sea in a storm, then after it started to capsize, people scrambled over one another as they tried to cling by their fingernails to the sides of the broken boat rolling in the waves, but none were able to hold on while being thrown against one another in the frenzy of the sea. When the boat fully capsized, all these terrified people were thrown into the sea, where they were washed back and forth like seaweed in the waves lashing a steep rocky coastline, where many drowned. Maybe, like so many before, and possibly tens of thousands more to come, the woman had one last chance to call out the name of the baby she had left behind. And maybe in those last moments as she sunk towards a watery grave among vast fields of seaweed, she realised that she had taught her child how to survive.

What were their names? Who were they? It makes you wonder. What were the names of all these people who were once the caretakers of their homelands through eras and epical stories, just as the land was once their caretaker?

Walls of barbwire, sheets of steel, bricks, stones, reinforced cement, and the prisons we construct in the mind to keep others out require constant vigilance. *They can't come here*. Godlike, we have become an army of watchers, to anxiously guard ourselves against a world of strangers. Privilege stares suspiciously out of self-erected watch towers to fend off the simple dreams to stay alive of sixty-five point three million globally displaced people in the world today. *Not on our watch,* we say. High noon needs a new time for every one person in one hundred and thirteen of the world's population, those millions escaping with their lives, those millions trapped for decades in refugee camps in a foreign country, those who are being persecuted, and those who are now roaming the planet in search of a haven, a place to be, to try to begin their lives again, or living in dreams of going home.

What was her name, then – the woman with the baby boy, and what was his name? What are the names of the world's homeless, the millions of people who need a new time? Do we know the special names given to these people by their families, clanspeople or tribes, who gave children names that meant something? Was it a name given as a blessing for the future, just like a baby girl would have been given a loved name way back in 1788 on the headlands of Botany Bay, or a baby given to a people-smuggler by an ill-fated mother who was given a moment to decide? Were all these millions of people given the learned names of centuries, a name meaning great gladness, or the person who looks after his clan, or a name meaning trustworthy, someone who is safe and worthy, or ray of morning sunlight, or to be a teacher, or to be fearless, or to be imaginative, or named after his beloved homeland where the sweetest dates or flowers grow? Or the name of an important flower of the mountains or deserts, or as a child of a sky God, hope, or tenderness, servant of God, power of the tribe, learned, a man of wisdom, to illuminate, a servant of compassion or a worshipper, dear to his people, friend, or a deer or gazelle, or of a beloved olive tree grove of the homeland, or forgiveness or generosity, or to illuminate, or called after a worthy character of the oldest fable in the land, or a beloved Goddess, or was she named for one who is worthy of praise?

地平線[01]の叙事詩

アレクシス・ライト

有満保江 訳

古代の風

目の前に広がる波は、私たちが頭の中に描く境界線を根こそぎ持ち上げ、運び去り続けてくれるだろう。嵐のように猛烈な勢いで過ぎていく時代の流れが、自分自身を閉じ込めていた心の中の壁を侵食し、打ち砕いてくれるだろう。まるでよそ者を排除するために張りめぐらされた有刺鉄線を破壊するかのように。私たちは海の中の魚に触れることができる。けれどそこには境界線はない。波の下に潜んでいて、すでに忘れ去られているどんな神でも、何に阻まれることもなく私たちの意志を波の下から押し上げてくれるだろう。私たちが呼吸する空気は、よそ者が呼吸する空気と混ざりあい、太古の昔からいつもその場所で吹いている風が、過去に捨て去ったさまざまな音の破片とともに、ガラクタ交響曲を生み出してくれる。そして私たちは皆、その音を聞くのである。

ある日のこと、この大陸南部のダルグ(エオラ)[02]族の言語でいう、またはワラン(シドニー湾)の水平線上に、白い幽霊たちが姿を現わした。彼らは越えてはならない土地の境界線を越えて向かってきた。昔から海岸線の守護霊である風の精は、幽霊たちが乗ってきた船のぬるぬるした船体の側面や、囚人たちの生気のない汚れた皮膚にその頬を押しつけた。風の精は船の隅っこや裂け目をするりと吹き抜けたときに死体のにおいを嗅ぎ、白い幽霊たちに恐怖心を抱いた。そしてその恐怖心は何かが起こる前触れとなり、やがて現実のものとなった。風の精は打ちひしがれた動物のように恐怖に慄き、後ずさりしながら逃げていった。老婆のように怒り狂った叫び声をあげながら、その場所を吹き抜けたという痕跡を残して立ち去っていった。風の精は猛スピードで海岸を上へ下へと吹き荒れ、穢れのない自分の肌を清めるために海面すれすれにヒューヒューと音をたてながら舞い、やがて突風となって移動中の蝶の大群を巻き込んでいった。

風の精は空高く舞い上がり、何千キロメートルもある大陸の周りを猛スピードで旋回し、自分が犯した冒涜のニュースを触れてまわった。すると最長老の先祖の霊は、ノース・サイクロンや強烈な突風を吹かせ、東の海岸線をぼろぼろにうち砕いてしまった。動乱の前触れなのだろうか、その広大な土地の上に広がる空間に、雷と稲光を乱舞させて大空をかき乱した。その間、白い幽霊たちが乗っていたそれまで見たこともない船は、波頭でゆらゆら揺れ動き、波の下に潜んでいた強靭な先祖たちは幽霊船をカタカタ鳴らせたり揺さぶりをかけたりした。船は魂がすっかり抜けてしまった屍のように、音をたてることもなかった。魂の抜け殻となった木造船は、船の本質ともいえるその魂を我われの先祖たちに引き渡すつもりはなかったのだ。その先祖たちこそがこの土地の最初の住人だというのに。船が侵入してきたことをめぐって、白い幽霊たちが先祖たちと意見を交換することはまったくなかった。先祖たちが耳にしたのは、ディン・ドーン・ディンという船のドラの音と、神の声とは程遠い何かを要求するだけの、聞いたこともない声だけだった。

この出来事こそが、最初の幽霊たちを運んできた11隻の船団の、8か月間にわたる船旅の叙事詩だった。この船旅は、はるか遠くのブリタニア[03]に始まった侵略のための航海だった。ブリタニアには、昔クロウと呼ばれた神の王であるブリテン王[04]のような祖先の神々がいて、武器を使って人びとを支配する方法を民衆に教えた。残虐で征服欲の強い人間たちは、血に穢れた鞭や銃を振りかざし船上を動きまわった。当時の戦争の神々は、人間を隷属させるために戦い、彼らの戦う方法は人間の血管の中を流れ、海の神であるマナナン・マクリル[05]の方法もまた、多くの囚人たちの血管の中を流れていったのである。

木造船は、流れるような曲線を描く大きな帆布に強い風を受けながら進んでいった。1788年1月26日、船には1336名の人間が乗っていた。彼らのほとんどは囚人で、11隻の船のうちのいくつかの船上の監獄に詰め込まれていた。ほんの微々たる、取るに足らない、それでも罰を逃れることのできない罪を犯した大勢の囚人たちが、故郷から遠く離れた地球の反対側に永遠に追放されたのだ。彼らはこの地に流刑植民地を築くために、鞭打ちの刑を受けながら労役を強いられた。遠く離れた彼らの本国にある政府と、この大陸に大英帝国女王の名のもとに設立された植民地政府はともに、当時この大陸には誰も住んでいないと信じ込んでいたし、その後もそう信じ続けた。なぜならば、そこに住んでいた人びとは、そう！黒人だったからである。その頃、黒人は人間以下だと信じられていたのである。

この大陸へ最初に侵入してきた人びと、そしてそのあとに続いてやってきた人びとが、この大陸に関する事実を、オーストラリアの高等裁判所を通じて認識するまでに二世紀という年月を要した。その事実とは、たとえばこの大陸全体を伝統的に所有していた人びとが、世界でもっとも高度に進化した法と洗練された政治制度をもっていたこと、そしてこの大陸全体が地上で最も巨大な法の大聖堂を形成する神聖な場所であり、彼らがこの神聖な場所を護り続けてきたということ、などである。この大陸は図書館だったのである。つまり、この大陸に関する知識は、古くから伝わる叙事詩的な物語として土地のなかに保管され、その物語はこの土地から生み出されているのである。この土地は想像を絶するほど巨大な知識の保管所であり、古くからこの土地に住む人びとが、この土地の様々な場所の自然や風景と霊的に交感することによって、この土地を護ってきたのである。

叙事詩的物語はこの大陸の根幹となる法でもあり、何千年ものあいだ神聖なものとされ、常に書き替えられてきた。そしてこの土地の守護者たちによって執り行われた儀式の中で読みあげられてきた。高度な宗教的秩序をもつこの土地の管理者である図書館員は、この土地に関して彼らの従属的な人びとが、あいかわらず「天地創造の時から」といっていたまさにその頃からずっと、この土地の知識を消すことなく保存してきたのだ。しかし悲しいことに、この知識の伝統的な所有者たちにとって、この侵略は決して止まることはなかったのである。その悲惨な結末のすべては今日まで続いている。

想像していただきたい。白い幽霊の船団がこの地に到着し、何百人という幽霊のような人びとが船を降り、ダルグの地の砂を踏むのを見たとき、ダルグの人びとがとてつもない衝撃を受けた日のことを。白い幽霊たちは、この場所の伝統的な法のもとに語られた力強い物語とは何の関係もなかったし、それに興味すら示さなかった。現在の世界の人口に置き換えて考えてみると、一万一千人という数の、それまで見たこともない人間が目の前に現れたことになるが、彼らがダルグの人びとの目にどのように映ったか、それは想像を絶するほどの衝撃だったに違いない。ダルグの人びとは、無知な白い幽霊たちのせいで、この土地の精霊たちが危険な存在になることはわかっていたのであろう。

土地に属することについて

白い幽霊船団が到着した時のことを想像していただきたい。伝統的なこの土地の所有者が、土地の統治に関するもっとも古い法物語について何を知っていたのかを。伝統的な法物語は、土地への帰属に関する膨大な知識から作られており、人びとの記憶の中に保管され、土地そのものから読み解かれるものである。先祖によって創造され、与えられ、保存され、絶えることなく代々伝達されてきたこの案内書が、世界でもっとも長く生き続けている文化の中にあることを想像してみてください。昔から語り継がれてきた知識のもとに土地を護りながら生きてきた人たちは、この土地のどんなささいなことでも、たとえば流れる水の動きの変化でさえも、その原因を突き止め解読してしまうのである。

はじめて白い幽霊たちと接触した人間が、土地の境界線の統治をめぐって、互いに脅しあう暴漢だったというのだろうか？膨大な数の戦士たちのために、膨大な数の槍を彫って侵略に備えたり、自分たちがこの土地に居座るために国土の周囲に石壁を築き、自分たち以外の人びとを追い出したりしたであろうか？あるいは、かわいそうな近隣国の沖合に拘留所を造って難民たちを生涯そこに監禁しようとしただろうか？いや、そんなことはありえない。先祖たちの物語は、そんな方法とは異なるやり方で人びとを導いてくれたのである。先祖たちの理論や思想は、法物語に基づいており、常に人びとにとって最も大切な先祖たちと同じ行動をするように導いてくれるものである。おそらくそれらは、土地を危険な状態から守り、また土地に活力を与えてくれる古い法を守っていくための知識を求めていくよう、また幽霊たちとの相互理解を求めていくよう、導いてくれるものである。

先祖たちは高度に洗練された土地に関する法をもち、その法によって物語が語られ、その物語の筋書きどおりに行動することが義務づけられていた。彼らは法の実践に精通し、この土地を護ってきた。彼らは代々伝えられてきた法に導かれて行動してきたのだ。高波が打ち寄せる海の物語をよく知っていたし、そよ風なのかそれとも蝶の群れが飛び交っているのか、空気感でその違いを識別できた。猛々しい嵐やすさまじい勢いでたたきつける雨まじりの突風の中にも、先祖たちが残してくれた物語を読み取ることができた。雨がまったく降らない旱魃の時も同様だった。彼らはいつもの習慣として海を観察する方法を知っていたのだ。彼らが規則的に歌う長い歌の繰り返しの中で、海にしばしば話しかけ、途方もない年数をかけて彼らに伝えてきたなじみの物語の中に法を読み解いていたのであろう。

伝統的にこの土地を所有する人びとは、海が荒れ狂っていたことにすでに気づいていたのだろう。おそらく帆船がこの地に上陸する数日前から、いや数か月も前から、彼らにはわかっていたのであろう。老婆はどうして大声で叫んでいるんだ、と先人たちはいいあっていたに違いない。海の上を吹くおだやかな風が、この時期になるとどんな動きをするのか、彼らにはわかっていた。なぜならば、先人たちと風の先祖とのあいだには密接な関係があったからだ。しかしそれよりも、大切に護られていた親戚や最愛の人が混乱し、おかしな行動をとりはじめたからだった。先人たちは、過去にこのようなことを経験したことはなかった。風雨にさらされた砂岩の絶壁に風が激しくたたきつけるときも、こんなことはなかった。その土地と大切な繋がりのある家族がキャンプをしていたところでは、囁くような声が聞こえた。そこから海を見わたす大気の中に白い幽霊たちをすでに見てしまった先人たちは、大地から姿を現してきて、そこでキャンプをしていた家族たちと一緒に、とんでもないことが起きるのではないかと待ち構えていたのだ。

彼らはその時すでに侵略の極悪非道さを、骨身にしみるほど感じとっていたのかもしれない。およそ尋常ではない摩訶不思議なことが起き、彼らの命にとって大切で本質的なものが身体の中から追い出されていくのを感じていたのだろう。ウォンガ鳩[06]が速いテンポでクークー鳴き続けていたのも、何か異変が起きていたことの証拠だったし、彼らがすでに影の人間、すなわち魂が抜けた存在になりつつあったのも不思議な出来事に違いなかった。ひどく無防備な状態であると感じながら、彼らは身体から追い出された自身の魂の本質を再び見つけ出すために、終わりの見えない未来を探らなければならない。そしてそれがどんなに大変であるかを、すでに感じていたのかもしれない。いつ鳴き止むともしれない鳩の鳴き声は耳にうるさく、心に不安を感じさせるものだった。年老いた男女はその不安を鎮めるために、自分たちの土地の霊に囁くような声でずっと話しかけていたのだ。この人たちは、木の上のほうで一晩中鳴いていた黒い頭と白い身体の精霊の鳥たちの鳴き声のせいでほとんど眠ることもできず、大変なことが起きそうな気がすると皆でいいあっていたのだ。彼らは、風の中で叫んでいる太古の精霊たちの声を聞いて鳴き止まない鳥たちを退散させて、非道な悲しみを克服しようと語りあっていたのだった。彼らにはわかっていた。彼らは常に何かが変化していることを感じ取っていたのだろう。どうしてこんなことが起こりえたのか—どうして古い法が破られたのか、不思議に思っていたのであろう。なぜなら、古くからある法を護るために先祖たちから引き継いできた義務を、自分たちは真面目に実践してきたと固く信じていたからだった。そしてこの法こそが、この力強い土地を数千年、数万年ものあいだ護り続けてきたのだと信じていたからだった。

奥地では、古いユーカリノキが強風でなぎ倒され、岩場の裂け目からシダが生えていた。そんな場所からは、数えきれないほど多種多様の鳥たちの鳴き声が聞こえてきた。たとえばスズドリにバタンインコ、色彩豊かな身体と美しい声をもつインコたち。その鳥たちの歌声は、最初は低い声から次第に甲高い声となり、夜明け前になると最高潮に達して大地に響き渡った。暗闇の中の鳥たちのコーラスはさざ波のような音に聞こえ、広大な奥地で繰り返され、やがて大陸の内部へと拡散していった。そして鳥たちのさえずりは波が押し寄せるように大陸全土を一周し、再びもとの場所にもどってくるのだった。背の高いユーカリノキの下には低木の茂みがあり、トカゲ、ヤモリ、ヘビ、その他の動物が棲息していた。また、そこには黄色の毛皮をまとったディンゴもいて、けたたましい鳥たちの鳴き声を聞いて何かがおかしいと感じとった。下生えにできた自分たちの通り道の上をゆっくりとした駆け足でその場を立ち去っていった。岩のあいだの奥まった場所にそっと身を隠すディンゴもいれば、神聖とされている洞窟の中に身体を小さく丸めて隠れるディンゴもいた。彼らは自分たちの隠れ場所の外側で起こっているものには目をつぶって、そのまま眠って過ごそうとしていた。

岬に住むダルグ族出身の、最も古いガーディガルフ・クラン[07]の人びとであるが、夜明け前だというのに黒い雄の嵐の鳥、つまりコエル・カッコー[08]の鳴き声を聞き驚いて目覚めたところだった。それから彼らは、その鳴き声がずっと遠くの場所にいる他のコエル・カッコーたちの鳴き声と反響しあっていることに気づいた。その反響音が即座にコエル・カッコーの物語を遠く離れた大陸の反対側に伝えるには、数千キロメートルもの海岸線を移動しなければならなかった。そのクランの人びとは、鳥のクォイ、クォイ、クォイという警告の鳴き声はあいさつの声でもあることを知っていた。そして彼らは暗闇の中では低くほとんど囁くような声で、ダラグの言語で話していた。霧が晴れ、湾に現れた白い幽霊の姿を見て、彼らはおそらく鳥たちが鳴いている現象は、海の先祖たちが戻ってきているからだと思った。彼らは、鳥たちの穏やかな鳴き声が不必要にかき乱されているようだと小声で話しあった。

それからほどなくして、彼らは海に現れた白い幽霊についての話をすることはなくなった。スワンプ・クーカル[09]のクー、クーという長く繰り返される悲しげな叫び声は、草原地帯や湿地帯から聞こえてくることもあった。その鳥の鳴き声が何かの予兆だということについては誰も語ることはなかったが、それは先祖の物語が警告をしているようなものだった。つまり何をすべきかの指示を与えてくれる先祖の物語のことを思いなさい、という警告だったのだ。鳥の鳴き声は、生まれたての赤ん坊に何か関係しているのだろうか、と彼らは考えたかもしれない。そのとき長老たちの頭をよぎったのは、成り行きに任せたほうがよいということだった。おそらく、彼らは警告については後で話すつもりだったのだろう。父親は、生まれたばかりの娘を抱き上げ、赤ん坊の先祖たちにお披露目をした。それから代々受け継がれている土地の創造者であるすべての先祖たちに見てもらえるように、赤ん坊は彫刻を施したクーラモン[10]の中に寝かされ、お祖母ちゃんに抱きかかえられた。長老たちは母親や赤ん坊たちと、まだほんの数時間前に生まれたばかりの新しい仲間をとり囲んでおしゃべりをしたり笑ったりしはじめた。彼らのクランに属する人びとは、子供たちにつける名前には、いつも土地に責任を負わせるような特別な意味をもたせるのだと話し合った。なぜならばそれが法だったからだ。

生まれたばかりのこの女の赤ん坊の名前はすでに知れ渡っており、長老たちにも認められていた。なぜならその名前は神聖な法に従うものであり、皆に愛される名前だったからである。また、この名前は昔からの知恵や意味を伝えるものであり、赤ん坊は法を守る責任と人びとを結びつける絆の役割を担っていた。それは、あたかも大陸全体を縦横無尽に駆けめぐり大陸をひとつに結びつける無数の連絡網のようだった。

夜が明けて間もないころ、キャンプファイアーから煙が立ちのぼり、その煙が奥地に広がっていく。すると母親たちが赤ん坊の名前を何度も何度も呼んだり囁いたりする声が風に運ばれてくる。その声は先祖たちの耳にも届き、やがて何世代にもわたる命の地図の記憶が子供のために形成される。早朝に赤ん坊の名前を呼んだり囁いたりすることによって、赤ん坊が生まれて最初に耳にする声が、その子供が属するクランの人びとの声だということを、母親たちが確認するのである。クランの人びとの多くは、朝日が出始めると岬に集まって、霧に包まれた水平線を見渡しながら風が吹くのを待っていた。幾人かの女性たちは波に向かって歌い、波を護る先祖の霊たちの話をして風を吹かせた。彼らはいつも法に従って行動していたように、鯨の家族がまもなく通り過ぎていくのをおそらく待っていたのだろう。岬では、そのあと男たちが出てきて鯨たちに挨拶をし、自分たちの精霊の旅についての話をし、それから鯨たちの物語を聞くのであった。それと同じように、このあたりを通りがかる他の仲間たちの話も聞くのであった。

その日の霧が晴れると、クランの人びとは海の景色が永久に変わってしまったことに気づいた。幽霊船が停泊し、やがて長い物語がはじまった。その物語は、どのようにして幽霊の数が増え続けたのか、そして幽霊たちがどのようにして戦争をはじめたのかについて語るものだった。幽霊たちが引き起こした戦争は、この大陸に古くから伝わるの歴史的記録の多くを破壊してしまった。それらは数万年ものあいだ、宗教的には高位にある守護霊たちによって神聖が保たれており、伝説にも語られているように、その守護霊たちにはこの土地を護っていく責任があったのである。

葦の記憶

身体は経験した物語を永遠に記憶している。襲撃され口を封じられた物語、逃亡して二度と帰還できなかった物語、故郷に二度と戻れなくなった物語、奴隷にされた物語、灼熱の太陽の下で木に縛りつけられ幾日も放置されたあげく、先端に有刺鉄線を括りつけた鞭で身体の皮膚がぼろぼろになるまでぶたれ続けた物語、レイプされた物語、自分の家族が殺された物語、抱きかかえる子供を腕からもぎ取らないで、と馬に乗った男たちに懇願する物語、赤ん坊を岩にぶつけて放り投げないで、殺さないで、と懇願する物語、土地を奪われその土地に伝わる物語を破壊された物語。これらの物語のすべては、身体が永遠に記憶している。迫害をどのようにして止めるか、自分の土地で害虫のように蔑まれることをどのようにして止めるか、これらを教えてくれる法が古文書にあるというのか？心は新規巻き返しができるけれど、身体は襲撃された記憶を、何世代も先の人びとの夢の中に伝えていくのである。

先人たちの物語が、こんなことを語ることがあるだろうか？たとえば、この世の中が、それ自体の逃亡を夢想したり、昔から伝え語られている土地や海の物語の中から消えてしまったこの世の中の管理人を探し出そうと、夢想したりすることがあるだろうか。大地の管理人は一体どうなったのかと、大地が夢想しなければならないのだ。この世の中が、精霊を失った影として夢想するというのか？この世の中が、精霊を失った場所にため息をつくというのか。

この大陸の古い伝統の中で生きてきた母親は、白い幽霊たちがこの土地を侵略したことを知ると、命がけでこの地を去ったであろう。世界の歴史の中には、数々の戦争によって家族から引き離された人びとが何百万人と存在するが、彼女もその一人だった。白い幽霊の男の集団が彼女の目の前で夫を殺したあと、彼女はその場から逃げ去った。自分の赤ん坊を抱きかかえ、無我夢中で湿原を駆け抜けた。それはかつて恐怖に怯えていた人びとが、海の神ネプチューン[11]の後を追ってアドリア海の塩水の湿原を命がけで逃げ惑い、ヴェネツィア・ラグーン[12]の水路と浅瀬にある小さな島々に身を隠したのと同じだった。土地を追われた先祖たちは、ワトル[13]や柳の若木が生えている高台に遊ぶ鳥たちのように、湿原で暮らしたのだった。

彼女と一緒に逃げた同じクランに属するおじいちゃん、おばあちゃん、赤ん坊を護ってくれた人びとは、何世代にもわたって同じクランの人びとから愛されてきたこの子供の名前が、神聖な場所の物語として遠く離れた時代の記憶になるだろうと、心の奥底でわかっていた。母親は、自分が何者でもなくなっていたことに気づいた。というのも彼女は何も感じなくなっていたからだった。彼女は自分が何をしているのかさえ分からなくなっていた。それに言葉は何の意味もなさない。彼女が逃れてきたこの場所を見て、この場所に伝わる物語に恐怖を覚え、音が口のなかで言葉にならなかったのである。彼女が属していたドリーミング[14]の場所から遠く離れたこの場所に、自分はいるべきではないと感じた。そこではもう、どんな物語も聞くことができなくなっていた。自分の赤ん坊の泣き声すら聞き取れなくなっていたのである。

自分の土地から逃れてきたこの場所で、音が聞こえなくなり、言葉を失い、生まれたばかりの赤ん坊を片腕でかかえながら腹ばいになって進んでいるうちに、彼女は現実には存在しない、影のない存在となってしまった。土地の低い、数キロメートルも続く湿地帯の中の、葦が生い茂っている場所を移動していた。ディンゴやゴアナに追いかけられ、葦の茂みに逃げ込んでいた昆虫たちの通ったあとを辿っていった。母親は夜になると水辺の葦の茂みにとどまった。赤ん坊は、母親が恐怖のあまり心臓をバクバクさせる音や、身体をガタガタ震わせている音を聞き、母親がすっかり言葉をなくしてしまったことを知った。母親は、自分の家族とともに身を隠しながら、あえて眠ろうとはしなかった。彼女は言葉を失うことによって警戒心が研ぎ澄まされ、手だけで会話をした。それというのも、隠れている母親は、隠れているイシチドリ[15]が雌の霊になっていくのを聞いたからである。危険を感じとり、灰色と茶色が混ざった羽のマントをまとった霊たちは、自分たちのハイピッチの鳴き声が、葦の生えている水辺の中に響き渡るように鳴き続けた。夜になると霊たちの死にまつわる物語を伝える声が、前に後ろにこだました。それから夜明けの霧の中に銃声が鳴り響くと、沈黙が訪れた。夜明けの大気の中に鳥の声は聞こえなくなった。その土地はまるでその先数百年にわたって、喪に服しはじめたかのように感じられた。

ツバメの家

彼女は飛び立った。あのツバメの少女が。娘の娘の娘の、その次の、またその次の娘のツバメが。はるか遠くのどこか別の場所から飛び立った。かわいそうな娘よ、それは一昔前のことだった。ツバメたちが作った精霊の家から巣立って、そして渡り鳥のように、今にも崩れそうなぼろぼろの壁に囲まれた巣を建て直すために、再び戻ってきたのだ。渡り鳥の長い飛行の準備を整えているとき、不安な旅のあいだに昆虫たちを追いかけるツバメたちのように、突然飛び込んでくる鷲たちから身をかわしながら、その娘の思いは空を駆け巡った。彼女にとって、渡り鳥としての飛行は命をかけるも同然だった。彼女は飛行しながらいったいどんなことを思ったのだろう？黒人のメイドとして働くのはもういやだ、とか？彼女は美しいレースで飾られた純白の舞踏会用のガウンを着て、家の影から文字通り飛び立ったのだろうか？そして警戒心のないすばらしい夢の明るい光の中で、自分を失ったのだろうか？その夢の明るい光は、輝きながら彼女の頭の中に流れ込んでいった。

彼女の頭の中で不確実なものがイバラのように大きくなっていった。その不確実な道を進むよう彼女の背中を押してくれたのは、このような明るい光の景色だった。しかしイバラの道は、彼女にとっての地平線の風景を封じ込めるために造られた、見通しのきかない深い藪だった。その道を通るとき、彼女がどうしてもできないことについて、ああしろ、こうしろ、と命じる声がした。たとえば、教えたとおりに、ベッドで眠りなさい、という声や、ベッドを使ったあと、きちんと完璧な形に整えなさいという声もした。その声は彼女が何の役にもたたない人間であることを告げていた。彼女が頭の中で想像できるもっとも小さな道具は希望だったのだが、その希望を携えて道を切り開いていくのは途方もないことだった。彼女は藪の中の茎をかき分けて、果てしなく続く暗闇の中のやわらかくて黄色い草地を通りぬけると、やがて最も不思議な世界へ入る道に辿り着いた。その世界は、作物が育てられている畑の向こう側の、すべての地平線から分離された、遠く隠れた場所にあった。その世界は彼女を監禁して労働を強いた、遠く離れた牧場主の屋敷の中にあった。彼女が働く台所の窓の外に何が仕掛けられているのか、およそ知るはずもない若い女性の夢を阻むものは、あまりにも多くの星が輝いている空だったのかもしれない。彼女はその窓に何年も立ち続け、その窓から地平線をずっと眺めたのだった。

それから彼女が一度、流れに身を任せて過ごしはじめると、この場所の悲惨な歴史が、その不思議な世界の中に、まるでがらくたのように途切れることなく放り込まれていった。このひとつの場所を知っているという感覚や、熟知しているこの悲しみに向かってツバメのように行ったり来たりと移動する感覚に、永遠に立ち戻っていくという彼女の思いは、どんなに距離が離れようとも止めることはできないであろう。これ以上ないほどに長い旅から戻ったあとで、彼女はゆっくりと崩れかけている家の周りを歩き、その壁の感触を白日夢のなかで何度も味わっていた。町の明るい光の中で、あの古い家がなんてすばらしくて静かであったことかと、彼女はしばしば話した。そしてまるで彼女が遠く離れた場所に立っているかのように、そこにいることがどんなに心地よいものかを感じていた。そこでは彼女はいつも大切にされていたと話した。まるでツバメが飛び回るように男たちと夜の街で踊りを踊った。彼女のドレスは、洗濯物を干す綱の上で風に大きくうねる布のように渦を巻いた。彼女はこの場所で、ツバメがぬかるんだ泥を集めて排水管へと飛んでいき、巣を作るために壁をせっせと補強しているのを食い入るように見つめた。

不思議な幻想の世界から、火傷しそうな熱いお湯で皿を洗うために台所の窓に戻るには、時間はそれほどかからなかった。それから鍋や釜についた油をゆっくりと時間をかけて落とした。その間、風に吹き飛ばされて切り株のようになった黄色い草原の風景に、灰色のホコリがたつのを眺めていた。その光景は彼女の内なる海で、彼女が地平線の向こう側で罠にかかっていたかつての自分たちのこまごまとした所有物を見つけるために、物語の記憶を探る旅に出ていたのだった。彼女の内なる海は、地平線から平らな広野を越えてもどってきた彼女自身の明確な世界観と、彼女自身とを結びつけてくれた。地平線の向こう側では、影が本当の意味での身体だ。[16]

この地平線という罠に再び捕らわれていると、かつて彼女がその昔知っていたかもしれない少女が馬の背に乗せられて家に運ばれてきたことを時々感じることがあった。彼女が時間を超越するという感覚に陥るのは、まさにこのような時だった。時間を超越するとは、物事が変化することがなく、物語だけが存在を実感させてくれる状況をいう。しかもその物語は交換可能な記憶の糸が無秩序に絡みあわさったものだった。彼女はこのことを堅く信じており、深い信仰心をもった礼拝所の人間であるということを感じた。この状況にあってこそ、彼女は永遠に穢れのない状態で幻想の中の自己を保つことができ、大地の土から収穫できる想像上の穀物を常に求めることができるのだった。そしてその土地の泥は、きちんとアイロンがかかって皺もない彼女の洋服に飛び散ってもそれを汚すことはないし、土地の刻印を残すこともなかった。彼女が台所の窓辺にいると、気分が高ぶった不寝番の感覚を必要とする永遠の覚醒状態に陥った。その状態で、彼女は未来を警戒するために、頭の中では決して解決できないもののために、過去が姿を現すのを待つのだった。

彼女は常に一人だった。たとえ街の賑やかな通りを歩いているときでも、かつての夢を保管しておく実体のない影の場所に閉じ込められていたのだ。活気あふれる大声が響きわたる中で、彼女は精霊のいる静かな家の中に囚われていたのだ。そしてその家がぼろぼろと崩れ落ちていくのをじっと眺めていた。一方ではその昔、幼い少女が自分の親族に付き添われることもなく、男たちの馬の背に乗せられ運ばれていくのを見たという話を保存しておくために、ツバメたちは自分の家の壁を補修しようとしていた。そしてその少女は…

ナイチンゲールが鳴く場所

もしもこの場所、生活、そして土地に縛られて身動きのとれない状態にあったというならば、彼女はすでに死んでいたのだ。しかしこれは完璧な謎だった。身体だけは残っていたのだから。時代が変わり、しかもまったく異なる世界の中で、あまりにも多くの世代に渡って逃走し続けた末に取り残されてしまったひとりの子孫が海をじっと眺めていた。彼女には抜け殻だけが残っていた。彼女の精霊はすでに消え失せていた。その精霊は昔のままで、人が生き続けていくために、さらに歩みを進めていくために、充分な養分を与えてくれるものだった。しかしその姿はもうそこにはなかった。とっくの昔に、彼女の頭から猛スピードでどこかに消え失せてしまっていたのだ。彼女は決して終わることのない争いに恐れ慄き、暴力から逃れるために壁の背後に隠れて影として生きていた。しかし問題は、大地との絆を失ってホームシックにかかった老いぼれた哀れな精霊が、這いつくばって再びもどってきたということだった。精霊は情に訴えてその女性に接し続ける以外に手の施しようがないことを、そして彼女を一人にしておくことができないことを知っていた。決して辿りつくことのできない地平線を目指して進む彼女自身の人生の旅の中で、そしてより厳しい歩みを続けるその放浪の旅の中で、ほとんど消えかけていた精霊は、一千回、何百万回と旅した砂漠の砂や小石、そして粘土質の道の上で、彼女を引っ張り続けたのだった。そしてついに波打ち際までやってきた。新しい人生に辿り着くために最終の水平線に向けての旅の次の地点に立ったとき、大海を横断するための安全な道を進んでいくために、彼らの先祖の神とは異なるさまざまな神々や不正を犯す人間たちを追い払ったり、ときには彼らとの交渉において密かに共謀したりしたのは、まさにこの精霊だったのである。

精霊よ、このまま進んで行け！大きな精霊たちに話をしに行くのだ。囁くようなたくさんの祈りが風に吹かれて海を横断する波の上に運ばれていった。波の下には、大西洋のポセイドン[17]のように忘れ去られた昔の神々たちが棲んでいる。祈りが届くように競い合っているうちに、そのいくつかの祈りは荒々しいネプチューンのところにも届くかもしれない。ネプチューンはフローレンスの泉の中で自分の大理石の海馬[18]と一緒に立っている。これらの祈りは、世界中の波止場で祈りを捧げた何百万もの人びとをひとつに繋いだであろう。地中海を横断しようとして、アフリカの活気のある大海の女神イエマヤ[19]、アグウェ[20]、あるいは大洋の支配者ユーキアンなどに祈りを捧げる人びとや、あるいは別の場所から、たとえば洪水を制した海の王の人魚の娘ススルが海流を変えた場所からは、波や海流を起こすサムンドラ、ヴェラモ[21]、嵐や暴風雨そして海の神である住吉三神[22]、それにスサノオノミコト[23]、ワタツミ[24]、ニョルズ[25]、永遠の海の神—ヴァルナ[26]や、今でも海の旅行者から何百万という祈りや線香が寺に捧げられている媽祖[27]などに祈りを捧げる人びとなどは、ひとつに繋がれるであろう。

次の物語では、人間が造り出した不毛の地で奴隷状態になりながらもこの地点へ辿り着くことができたのも、また、その途中で多くの命が危険な人びとの手にかかりながらも安全な場所に行きつくことができたのも、数えきれない人びとのおかげだった、ということが語られている。きしみ音を響かせ、どこか別世界のように見えた波止場で待っているとき、彼女の頭の中はあの早朝の霧のようにふわふわと漂っていた。そこは魚や海のにおいが鼻につく場所、釣り人が海の神に向けて放った魚の骨を捕まえようとやせた猫が足をこすっている場所、暗闇に浮かぶ建物の屋上に並んで見える煙突から、ナイチンゲールの悲しげな子守唄が聞こえてくる場所だった。そのかたわらで、人びとは密輸業者とこっそり列をなして並び、航海に耐えられそうもない船に乗り込もうとしていた。その小さなナイチンゲールは旅の叙事詩を歌っている。東南アジアに向けて数千マイルを移動する旅、ヨーロッパ人の数を満たすためにヨーロッパに向かう旅、越冬のために青空を求めてサブ・サハラアフリカ[28]へ帰還する旅。ナイチンゲールは昇ってくる太陽の光のなかで止まることもなく、誰にも聞かれることもなく歌い続けた。その女は、船や釣ボートに乗るために何百年にも渡って使い続けてきたこの安全な波止場を虚ろな目で眺めていた。そんな時でも、ナイチンゲールの鳴き声は止むことはなかった。かつてその鳴き声は、収穫の時期や種まきの時期を知らせてくれたり、夜には埋葬された夫の息遣いの記憶を蘇らせてくれたりした。しかし、そんな鳴き声を聞いていた頃から随分時間がたってしまった。鳥の鳴き声は彼女にとってもう何の意味もなさなくなっていた。彼女は、先祖が伝説を語ってくれた場所から遠く離れた別の場所の夢の中にいた。そして彼女自身の人生とともに形成してきたもうひとつの伝説の中に、忘却の中に沈んで決して存在しない彼女の物語の中にいたのである。

この波止場で風と戯れながら、じっと見つめてはいるが実際には何も見ていない彼女にとって、安全というものはなかった。彼女は男の赤ん坊を強く抱きしめていた。そのとき彼女は、自分と赤ん坊が将来離れ離れになることをすでに感じ取っていた。赤ん坊は、まるで母親から離れようとしているかのように、落ち着きがなかった。赤ん坊は母親を忘れようとしているかのようだった。なぜならば、赤ん坊はまるで母親の腕から飛び立ちたいとでもいうように、自分を母親から引き離そうとしていたからだった。

赤ん坊の精霊は、パピリオに向かって進んでいった。パピリオは黒白のツバメのしっぽをもった蝶で、故郷に集まっていた人びとの背後で飛んでいるのを赤ん坊は見かけたのだ。おそらく同胞の人びとが故郷を去っていくので別れを告げにきていたのであろう。別れのときになると、大勢の人たちは彼らを待ち受けていた釣り用のボートに黙って乗り込みボートを満杯にした。そのボートは古いものでかつて老水夫が所有していたのであろう。赤ん坊は、彼をしっかりと抱いている母親の腕から反り返るような姿勢になっていた。それはまるで赤の他人が赤ん坊のぬくもりを求めて身体を引き寄せ、抱きしめているようだった。赤ん坊は先祖の伝説にでてくる蝶を追い、通りの暗がりに向かって飛び立とうと、身体をよじったりひねったりした。その通りは、何万という祖国を失った人びとが生きる場所を求めてひしめきあっていた。まるでその蝶が、赤ん坊がよく知っている生活の場所に赤ん坊を引き戻そうとしているかのように見えた。その場所は、サイクロンによって廃れていた街がズタズタにされ、一時しのぎの生活の中に釣り用のボートが放り込まれたようなところだった。

赤ん坊はすでに、彼の住居のドアの間を吹き抜ける昔の風のようだった。その住居は、荷造り用の箱を釘でぞんざいに打ち付け、プラスチックと薄鋼板をロープや針金で縛ってこしらえたものだった。母親がたった一人で赤ん坊を産むために見つけたこの場所は、難民たちが長い列をなして逃げだそうとしていた廃墟だった。この子は、道端で兵士たちによってレイプされて孕んだ赤ん坊だったのだ。頬と顎を互いにすり合わせるほどぎゅうぎゅう詰めにされ、威嚇され支配される空間で生きている何千人もの人びとがたてる騒音が、赤ん坊にとってのゆりかごだった。この場所こそが彼の家であり、家族を感じさせるところだった。また彼を寝かしつけてくれる音を感じさせるところでもあった。恐らく母親は、海の音が赤ん坊の心を乱していたことを知っていたのであろう。神様が赤ん坊にすでに話かけてくれていた。そして彼女はすでに一人きりで旅をしていたのだ。海が彼女を護ってくれる家となっていた。彼女は、何千マイルもの距離を移動してきた船やボートの動きを感じ取っていた。何万人もの人びとが、まるで動物が群れをなして荒廃した砂漠から逃げるかのように、船やボートに乗り込んでいたのだった。

自分たちが吸っているたばこの煙に隠れている男たちは、人の命を取引するあいだは冷静な行動をとる。彼らが彼女に何か月もの間いい続けているのは、もし彼女がうまく立ち回りさえすれば、彼らは彼女をなんとしてでも助けてあげたいと思っている、ということだった。彼らは彼女の話は予言だ、ばくちの運命だといっていたが、結局彼女は代価を支払い、霧のなかに停泊している壊れかけの釣り用のボートにたったひとつのチャンスを賭け、それに半分乗りかかっている状態だった。波止場にあるたったひとつの街灯のぼんやりとした靄の中で、彼女は妄想の世界に入ってしまっている。誰もかもが混乱状態で船に乗り込もうとしている一方で、彼女はすでにパニック状態に陥っている。なぜならば、この期に及んで人びとはなんとかボートに乗ろうともがいているが、もはやこれ以上、ボートには人を乗せる余裕はないと、彼女は内心わかっていたからだった。

彼女は、立ったまま押し合いへし合いしている何百人もの人びとの顔をじっとながめている。彼らも彼女を、限界を超えるほど混みあっているボートからじっと見つめている。安全だと感じられるものは何もない。しかし彼女はほかになす術もなく、チャンスがあるなら行くしかないということも知っている。彼女の金は支払われた。彼女にはもう支払う金はなかった。急げ！急げ！ばかだな！早く乗るんだよ、という声が聞こえる。彼女にはこの機会を逃すことはできなかった。ボートに乗るためにどっと流れ込む人びとの中の誰かが彼女をボートのほうに押したのを感じる。彼女にはもう時間がないという瀬戸際で、所持品が入った包みを片腕に、そしてもう片方の腕に赤ん坊をしっかりと抱きかかえようとする。そしておそらく、まだボートに乗っていない彼女やその他の人びとを見つめている人びとの、自暴自棄になっている表情の中に、彼女は、ボートを揺らしているのはこの土地の古代の神にちがいないとすでに感じとっていた。

大勢の人びとがボートに詰め込まれて、みな落ち着きなく立ったまま強く押し合っている。この人たちは、声にならない恐怖の叫び声をあげているのが彼女にはわかる。彼らのことを記憶していない海の神の向こう側へ進んでいこうとするこの旅のことを、彼らはすでに予見しているのだろう。彼女は逃げる者の本能として、ボートに乗り込んでぎゅうぎゅう詰めになっている彼らが、故意に舟を右に左にと揺さぶり、彼女がボートに乗れないようにするだろうと直感的に感じとっていた。ボートはすし詰め状態だった。彼女は、身体じゅうでこのことを理解していた。そしてちょうどその時その場所で、多くの手がボートから彼女に届くであろうことを知っていた。彼女がボートに乗り込もうとすると、その手が彼女と赤ん坊を波止場から落としてしまうことを、そして彼女と赤ん坊が真っ暗闇の海に落ちてしまうであろうことを知っていた。

黙って運命の決断を下したとき、彼女は突然パニック状態に陥り、ボートの両側に波がひたひた打ち寄せる音以外に、おそらく何も聞こえなくなっていたのだろう。汚職にまみれた警官によって彼女が乱暴にボートに押し込まれたとき、遠くに霧笛の音と船の鐘の音が波の大きなうねりの中で揺れるように聞こえた。この警官は清廉潔白と記録されてはいるものの、「大海の神」といった類のどこかの旅行代理店からすでに料金を受け取っていた。まるで担当区域を誰かに監視されてでもいるかのように、最後に舟に乗せる人間については気づかれないようにしようと決めていたのだ。彼女のほうは、大勢の人間が彼女をボートに乗せないよう手を伸ばしていたため、ほんの一瞬閃いた考えで彼女の残りの人生を決断するようにと強いられていた。その考えとは、何気ないおしゃべりのなかでもれ聞いたある噂についてだった。かつてユダヤ人たちが渡航中にひどい仕打ちを受けていたという噂が広がっていた。彼らが受けた仕打ちとは、今まさに彼女が受けているものと同じだった。彼女は、波止場の下で死んだ人びとが、ある神によってぞんざいに扱われているのを想像するのだった。その神は、これらの人びとが誰なのかを見極める手がかりを持たなかったのである。彼女と同じように、かつて地球上の人びとがそれぞれ渡航中に、はるかかなたの海で死んでしまい、航海を成し遂げられなかったことについて彼女は思いを馳せるのだった。

その考えは一瞬にして終わってしまった。彼女自身と赤ん坊が、混みあっているボートに乗り込もうとして海に落ちていく姿を彼女ははじめて考えてみた。自分と赤ん坊は、世界のどこかのたった一部にしかすぎない白い幽霊の神の、海藻が絡み合ったケルプの森の中で死んでしまった人間のようだった。ケルプとは、ポシドニア・オセアニカ、つまり海底の牧草地を構成し、波止場の下にも浮遊している海藻である。海上にいる人びとは半分浸水している船体の上で落ち着きなく立ちながら、ボートをまるで赤ん坊の揺りかごのように揺らし続けていた。ボートは不安定に左右に揺れ、生きるか死ぬかという決断をする間もなく前に進ませる最後の一押しがなされた場所で、一か八かの瞬間、ボートから落ちてしまうかもしれない自分を何かにつかまらせて安定させ、子供にいかに生き残っていくかについて教えることもできず、彼女は赤ん坊を警官に手渡してしまった。警官はそのときすでに波止場から暗い海にボートを押し出していた。

不寝番

何百人もの人間が壊れた古い釣り用ボートに乗っていたと人はいう。そのボートは嵐の海の中で手の施しようのないほど傾きはじめていた。ほどなくしてボートは転覆し、波にのまれて壊滅してしまった。船体の両側に指の爪で縋りつこうとしたときに乗っていた人びとの身体が重なりあって逆巻く波の中に放り出され、彼らは互いの身体にしがみつくことすらできなかった。ボートが完全にひっくり返ったとき、恐怖に晒されていたすべての人びとは海に投げ出され、身体はまるで海藻のように前に後ろにと波に漂い流されていった。その波は切り立った岩だらけの海岸線に勢いよく砕け散り、多くの人びとがそこで溺れてしまった。おそらく過去に多くの人びとがそうであったように、そして今後も何万人とさらに増えていくかもしれないが、その女性には置き去りにした赤ん坊の名前を呼ぶ最後のチャンスがあった。海藻が漂う広大な海床の中にある水中の墓場に向かって沈んでいく最後の瞬間に、彼女は自分自身が子供に、いかに生き残っていくかについてすでに教えていたことを認識したのだった。

彼らの名前は何だったのだろうか？彼らは誰だったのだろう？こんな疑問がわいてくる。いくつかの時代を経た叙事詩の物語の中で、かつて彼らの土地が彼らを護ってきたように、彼らはかつて彼らの故郷の地を護ってきたのだが、彼らすべての人びとの名前は何だったのだろうか？

有刺鉄線の壁、鋼板、レンガ、石、補強セメント、他人を追い出すために頭の中に築いた檻などは常に監視を必要とする。他人はここには来れない。我々をよそ者の世界から護るために、我われ自身があたかも神であるかのように、監視のための軍隊となったのだ。軍隊の特権で、我われが自分で建てた監視塔から、今日、世界中に存在する六千五百三十万人もの難民たちの生き続けようというシンプルな夢を護るために、疑い深く監視しているのである。我われの監視は逃れられない、と我われはいう。世界の人口の 113 人にひとりの割合で、新しい時代への最後の決断が迫られている。これら何百万人もの人びとは、外国の難民キャンプで何十年間も捕らわれの身で過ごしているのだ。彼らは迫害され続けた人びとであり、安息所となる場所を求めて惑星を放浪している人びとである。再び自分たちの自立した生活をはじめたり、故郷に帰ることを夢見たりしている人びとである。

それでは、彼女の名前は何だったのだろうか？あの男の赤ん坊を連れた女性の名前と赤ん坊の名前は？世界中のホームレスの人びとの名前は？新しい時代を必要としている何百万人もの人びとの名前は？これらの人びとや家族、同じ部族、あるいは同じ種族の人びとによって与えられた何か特別な意味のある名前を、我々は知っているだろうか？彼女の名前は、将来を祝福されるものとして与えられた名前なのだろうか？ちょうど 1788 年にボタニー・ベイで、愛されているという意味の名前が与えられた女の赤ん坊のように。あるいは、決断を下すのに一瞬しか時間が与えられなかった不運な母親によって密輸業者に預けられた赤ん坊のように。これら何百万人という難民は、何世紀にもわたって賢い人間としての名前が付けられているのだろうか？たとえば大きな喜びを表す名前、一族の面倒を見た人という意味の名前、信頼できるという意味をもつ名前、安全で価値のある人という意味の名前、朝の太陽の光を意味する名前、将来教師になる人の名前、恐れ知らずの、想像上の、といった意味の名前が付けられていたのだろうか？最も甘いナツメヤシや花が生育する愛する故郷にちなんでつけられた名前だっただろうか。山や砂漠に咲く大切な花の名前、空の神の子供としての希望ややさしさを表す名前、神に仕える人、部族の中で権力のある人、博識な人、知恵のある人、思いやりや崇拝者の使徒、あるいは同族の人びとや友人にとって大切な人、故郷の大切なオリーブの木立や、赦しと寛大さを照らし出す名前。あるいは、その土地の最も古い神話の中の尊敬すべき人物に光を当てる名前、その人物にちなんだ名前、大切な女神の名前、そして賞賛に値する人物のための名前が与えられていたのだろうか？

注

01　英語の horizon には「地平線」と「水平線」の両方の意味が含まれている。当翻訳では、horizon を文脈によって両者を使い分けている。

02　ダルグ（Darug）：植民地以前に現在のシドニーあたりに同族の集団で居住していた先住民の子孫。エオラ（Eora）はダルグの英語名。

03　ブリタニア（Britannia）：イギリス、特に古代ローマの属州ブリタンニアがあったグレートブリテン島南部の古称。

04　ブリテン王（Brân the Blessed）：ウェールズ神話にでてくるブリテンの巨大な王。

05　マナナン・マクリル（Manandán mac Lir）：アイルランドの伝説に登場する海の神。

06　ウォンガ鳩（Wonga pigeons）：豪州産の大型の鳩。

07　ガーディガルフ・クラン（Gadigal clans）：オーストラリアの先住民の人びとは「クラン」と呼ばれる親族集団で形成されていた。部族、氏族、一族などと表記されることがある。

08　コエル・カッコー（Koel Cuckoo）：アジア、オーストラリア、太平洋に生息するカッコー属の鳥で大きな声で鳴く。

09　スワンプ・クーカル（Swamp Coucal）：アフリカ、南アジア、オーストラリアなどの沼地に生息する鳥。カッコー科に属する。

10　クーラモン（Coolamon）：オーストラリア先住民の用いる木製、または樹皮製のたらい型の皿。

11　ネプチューン（Neptune）：ギリシャ神話の海の神で、ゼウスに次ぐ圧倒的な強さを誇る。海洋のすべてを支配する。怒り狂うと強大な地震を引き起こし、世界を激しく揺さぶる。泉の守護神ともされる。

12　ヴェネツィア・ラグーン（Venetian Lagoon）：ヴェネツィアの潟湖。アドリア海北部の潟のひとつでヴェネト州の海岸沿いにある。

注

13 ワトル（wattle）：豪州産アカシア属の高（低）木で、黄金色の花はオーストラリアの国章とされている。

14 ドリーミング（Dreaming）：先住民の思想や世界観を表し、太古の昔から受け継がれている神話物語で、土地と密接にかかわっている。

15 イシチドリ（stone-curlews）：鳥類チドリ目の 1 科である。 基本的に水鳥であるチドリ目には珍しく、水辺でない陸地に住む。

16 作者注：エリザベス・ビショップ（Elizabeth Bishop）の詩『不眠症』（Insomnia）からの引用。poemhunter.com。

17 ポセイドン（Poseidon）：ギリシャ神話の神で海の支配者。ローマ神話のネプチューンにあたる。注 11 を参照。

18 海馬（sea-horses）：ギリシャ神話にでてくる馬頭魚尾の怪獣。

19 イエマヤ（Yemaya）：ナイジェリア南西部の民族ヨルバ人の神話に登場する水の女神。

20 アグウェ（Agwe）：ハイチのヴードゥー教の海の神。

21 ヴェラモ（Vellamo）：フィンランド神話の水、湖、海の女神。

22 住吉三神：日本の神話で航海を守護する海の神。

23 スサノオノミコト：日本神話に登場する、多彩な性格を有する神。

24 ワタツミ：日本神話の海の神。

25 ニョルズ（Njord）北欧神話に登場する海を司る神。

26 ヴァルナ（Varuna）：古代インドの最高神。

27 媽祖（Mazu）：中国の女神で、航海・漁業の守護神。

28 サブ・サハラアフリカ（sub-Saharan Africa）：サハラ以南のアフリカ。

致谢

谨向李尧教授和有满保江教授致以深切的谢意，并感谢他们在翻译我的中篇小说《地平线上的奥德赛》的过程中表现出的洞察力和奉献精神。没有他们的热情和坚持不懈的支持，这个独特的、多语种的项目永远不可能进行下去。

我这部中篇小说最初是作为一本书的一部分出版的，这本书还与国际知名的澳大利亚艺术家特雷西·莫法特的展览同时出版。该展览在2017年第五十七届威尼斯双年展中展出。

参展的书由娜塔莉·金编辑，澳大利亚 Thames & Hudson 出版公司出版。

我要感谢澳大利亚理事会的慷慨支持，使我有机会对该出版物做出贡献。

我不无自豪地承认，我的女儿莉莉·萨文克在制作《地平线上的奥德赛》的美术作品和布局上展示了她出色的平面设计能力。

电影制作人兼摄影师安德烈·萨文克提供了澳洲鹤在卡彭塔利亚湾跳舞的标志性图像。书中出现的所有其他图片都是我自己的创作。

衷心感谢北京乐府文化和东京现代企画出版社。感谢他们为本书出版所做的大胆尝试和开拓创新。希望它能被广泛的读者接受。

亚历克西斯·赖特

ACKNOWLEDGEMENTS

I would like to express my gratitude and admiration to Professor Li Yao and Professor Yasue Arimitsu for their insight and dedication in the translation of my novella, *Odyssey of the Horizon* into Chinese and Japanese. Without their enthusiasm and ongoing support, this unique multi-lingual project may never have proceeded.

My novella was first published as part of a book which accompanied an exhibition by the internationally re-nowned Australian artist, Tracey Moffatt. Her exhibition was held at the 57th International Art Exhibition, La Biennale di Venezia, in 2017.

The exhibition book was edited by Natalie King, and published by Thames & Hudson, Australia.

I would like to thank the Australia Council for generously supporting my contribution to that publication.

I am proud to acknowledge that my daughter Lily Sawenko has demonstrated her outstanding graphic design skills in producing the artwork and layout for *Odyssey of the Horizon*.

The iconic image of the brolgas dancing in the Gulf of Carpentaria was provided by film maker and photographer, Andre Sawenko. All other photo images which appear in the book are my own.

My sincere thanks go to Pan Press Ltd, Beijing, and Gendai Kikakushitsu, Tokyo, for their bold and innovative commitment to the publication of this book. I hope it will be well received by the widest possible audience.

Alexis Wright

謝辞

私の中編小説『地平線の叙事詩』を中国語と日本語に翻訳をして下さった、リ・ヤオ教授と有満保江教授に、それぞれの洞察力と献身に対し、感謝と称賛の意を表したいと思います。お二人の熱意と、今なお途切れることのない支持なくしては、この類まれな複数言語による小説の翻訳出版の企画は実現しなかったと思います。

私のこの中編小説は、国際的に知られたオーストラリアのアーティスト、トレイシー・モッファト氏の展覧会の開催に伴い出版された書籍の一部として、初めて世に出ました。モファット氏の展覧会は２０１７年に、第５７回国際芸術展覧会、ラ・ビエンナーレ・ディ・ヴェネツィア展覧会として開催されました。その時の書籍は、ナタリー・キングによって編集され、テームズ・アンド・ハドソン・オーストラリアによって出版されました。

この書籍への私の寄稿に際し、オーストラリア・カウンシルより寛大なる支援と貢献を賜わりました。深く御礼を申し上げます。

また、この度の『地平線の叙事詩』という作品の出版に際し、グラフィック・デザインとレイアウトの技術を遺憾なく発揮し、すばらしい芸術作品を生み出してくれた、私の娘であるリリー・ソゥエンコを誇らしく思い、その貢献に謝意を表します。

カーペンタリア湾でダンスをしているブロルガ（鶴科に属するオーストラリアの鳥）の象徴的なイメージは、映画製作者でありまた写真家でもある、アンドレ・ソゥエンコによって提供されたものです。この作品の中で使用されたその他の写真は、すべて私自身が撮影したものです。

最後に、北京のパン・プレス、そして東京の現代企画室に対して、この本の出版への大胆で革新的な、そして惜しみない貢献に、深く感謝の意を表したいと思います。この本が多くの人びとに読まれ、そして歓迎されることを心より願っています。

アレクシス・ライト

译后记

2009年，澳大利亚著名作家尼古拉斯·周思（Nicholas Jose）先生推荐我翻译刚获得澳大利亚最高文学奖——“迈尔斯·富兰克林文学奖”的长篇小说《卡彭塔利亚湾》。他告诉我，这本书的作者亚历克西斯·赖特（Alexis Wright）是具有华人血统的澳大利亚原住民。她不但是知名作家，还是为澳大利亚原住民的利益奔走呼号多年的著名社会活动家。《卡彭塔利亚湾》更是一本不可多得的优秀小说，非常值得翻译成中文在中国出版。我对澳大利亚原住民文学和历史早已情有独钟，欣然接受周思的建议，着手翻译这本洋洋洒洒四十万字的长篇小说。但我首先想对亚历克西斯·赖特有所了解，赖特也非常热情地向我介绍了自己：她的曾外祖父是清朝末年从广东到澳大利亚北领地谋生的华人。这个亚历克西斯·赖特直到2009年还不知道姓甚名谁的中国男人流落到澳大利亚原住民居住的卡彭塔利亚湾，与赖特的曾外祖母相爱成家，生下五个孩子，三男两女。后来曾外祖父带着三个儿子回到中国，把妻子和两个女儿留在卡彭塔利亚湾，再也没有踏上澳大利亚那块遥远的土地。曾外祖父虽然从此杳无音信，但包括亚历克西斯·赖特在内的这个中国男人的后裔，始终认为他们具有华人血统，他们的根有一半在中国。赖特曾经对我说："曾外祖父的故事在我们这个大家庭里充满想象和传奇的色彩。那种骨肉分离、'家族树'被拦腰斩断的伤痛，就像一盏长明灯，照耀着后人。我们一代又一代卡彭塔利亚湾人持续不断地谈论这段历史，构成心理探究的一部分。"赖特在这盏长明灯的照耀下，执着地寻根问祖。经过艰苦的努力，她终于从维多利亚州档案馆里找到和她曾外祖父有关的材料。2013 年，我到墨尔本访问，她满怀喜悦地让我看她发现的曾外祖父"护照"上拖着辫子的照片（正面和侧面），还有一张一百多年前有他签名的工资条，上面赫然写着"徐三保"三个字。我告诉她，她的先人叫徐三保，她的根在广东省开平县。赖特听了欣喜若狂，紧紧地拥抱着我，仿佛我是他久别的亲人。那一天我们沿着巴拉腊特湖走了好久，眺望着碧蓝的湖水，她的眼角湿润，心思飘到遥远的北半球。2017 年，亚历克西斯·赖特应邀到广州参加"第四次中澳作家论坛"，我也有幸出席这次盛会。会议正式开幕前，在当地政府有关部门的帮助下，她和她的丈夫托里专程到离广州不远的开平县三桂里寻根，在徐家祠堂祭祖，还得到一部族谱。那部厚厚的族谱上虽然没有曾祖父的名字，但她仍然奉若传家之宝。她在祠堂点燃一炷香，祭奠先人；在乡亲家的灶台前小坐，品一盏新茶，那惬意的样子，仿佛是跋涉许久，终于回家歇歇腿的孩子。

亚历克西斯·赖特不但对中国这块热土怀有深厚的感情，对中国文学，特别是当代文学也有着浓厚的兴趣。她多次在中国、澳大利亚和中国作家交流，和铁凝、莫言、余华、阿来、张炜等作家多有交集。赖特说："对我而言，向中国作家学习是一件很重要的事情。有一首诗，我经常和我的朋友们分享。这首诗就是北岛的《播种者》，'一个念头让我发疯，他正在大理石上播种。'优美的诗句不时在我的脑海里回响，因为它告诉我们文字的力量，它可以与世界上任何一个地方、任何一个人对话。将人类联系起来的共同纽带，是永远不要忘记滋养我们的土地，不管生活在这个星球的什么地方。"

亚历克西斯·赖特就是怀着对这个星球炽热的爱，对脚下土地深深的感激，创作出一部又一部震动澳洲文坛的佳作。堪称民族史诗的长篇小说《卡彭塔利亚湾》中文译本，2012 年由人民文学出版社出版。这本书植根于澳大利亚原住民生活的沃土之上，把古老的传说、神话以及原住民信奉的“梦幻时代”的原始图腾和现实生活的种种矛盾糅合在一起，描绘出一幅幅难得一见、色彩瑰丽的画卷。在她的笔下,原住民生活的地方到处都是故事。每一眼水井、每一块岩石、每一座沙丘、每一棵树木都是故事中的“人物”。蛇神、海怪、鱼群、鹦鹉、巨浪滔天的大海、拔地而起的龙卷风都有独特的含义。而可以与《卡彭塔利亚湾》比肩而立的是她于 2015 年出版的另外一部巨著《天鹅书》（*The Swan Book*）。这部小说故事情节扑朔迷离,集诗歌、散文、民间故事、政论文等多种体裁于一身，对大自然的描写出神入化，对天鹅的刻画美妙绝伦。《天鹅书》的故事发生在未来一百年之后的澳大利亚北领地。小说的主人公哑女与天鹅相依为命，被称为“天鹅女”。“天鹅女”具有象征意义。作为一个无辜的弱小者，她遭受暴力之后不再说话，也渐渐失去说话的功能。这与澳大利亚原住民几百年来的遭遇如出一辙。作者之所以选取哑女作为原住民的象征，是因为她相信，他们根本无法发声。哑女与人类社会隔膜，却和天鹅相依为命，象征着原住民与大自然的紧密联系。2017 年，亚历克西斯·赖特的长篇纪实文学《追踪者》（*The Tracker*）出版，好评如潮，获 2018 年澳大利亚最重要的女性文学奖“斯特拉奖”（Stella Prize）。

2019 年，我到东京参加“日本澳大利亚研究国际学术研讨会”。来自世界各地的学者发表多篇论文对亚历克西斯·赖特的作品研究探讨，给我留下深刻的印象。恰在此时，赖特的新作《地平线上的奥德赛》（*Odyssey of the Horizon*）出现在我的视野。这篇充满诗意的散文虽然篇幅不长，却是震撼人心的佳作。该文以诗一般的语言叙述了 1788 年，英国“幽灵船”穿越地平线，入侵悉尼湾的故事；以痛彻心扉的呼喊唤醒暴力殖民的创伤性记忆；以悲愤交加的笔触书写了“世界历史上数以百万计饱受战争摧残的人”的迁徙，包括无数难民儿童遭受的苦难。这些生动的画面在赖特的作品中相互交织，有着强烈的现实意义。我突发奇想，可否把这篇深邃优美的散文翻译成中文和日文，与原文合成一集出版，创造一种新的模式，让亚历克西斯·赖特的作品走向更广阔的世界？会议期间，我和日本著名翻译家有满保江教授谈及这个想法，她欣然同意，同我一拍即合。亚历克西斯·赖特更是全力支持，不但无偿赠予我们这部作品的出版权，而且提供了她同时作为摄影艺术家多年来积累的表现卡彭塔利亚湾自然风情的图片。与此同时，我们邀请亚历克西斯·赖特的女儿、平面艺术设计师莉莉·萨文克为本书做美术装帧。就这样，中、日、澳三国文学艺术工作者怀着满腔热情，紧锣密鼓，打造这本希望是精品的小书。而在此过程中，乐府文化的各位年轻编辑表现出的热情，更令人感动。在新冠病毒肆虐的那个季节，他们不畏艰难，始终和我保持密切联系。我们心往一处想，劲往一处使，终于使得这条满载友谊和爱的小船到达胜利的彼岸。值此《地平线上的奥德赛》出版之际，谨向他们致以深切的谢意。

中文译者李尧

2020 年 9 月 26 日，写于北京

作者简介
About the Writer
著者について

—

亚历克西斯·赖特
Alexis Wright
アレクシス・ライト

亚历克西斯·赖特是卡彭塔利亚湾南部高原瓦伊族(Waanyi)的成员，是获奖小说《卡彭塔利亚湾》和《天鹅书》的作者。赖特还出版过三部非虚构作品：《像这位老人一样夺取权力》——中央土地理事会口述历史、《格罗格酒之战》——关于北领地酗酒的调研、《追踪者》——关于原住民领袖特里克·泰尔茅斯的集体回忆录。她的著作在包括中国、美国、英国、印度、意大利、法国和波兰在内的世界各地出版。目前她是墨尔本大学文学学院讲席教授(Boisbouvier Chair)。赖特是唯一同时获得迈尔斯·富兰克林文学奖(《卡彭塔利亚湾》, 2007年)和斯特拉奖(《追踪者》2018年)的澳大利亚作家。

·

Alexis Wright is a member of the Waanyi nation of the southern highlands of the Gulf of Carpentaria. The author of the prize-winning novels *Carpentaria* and *The Swan Book*, Wright has published three works of non-fiction: *Take Power Like This Old Man Here*, an oral history of the Central Land Council; *Grog War*, a study of alcohol abuse in the Northern Territory; and *Tracker*, an award-winning collective memoir of Aboriginal leader, Tracker Tilmouth. Her books have been published widely overseas, including in China, the US, the UK, India, Italy, France and Poland. She is the Boisbouvier Chair in Australian Literature at the University of Melbourne. Wright is the only author to win both the Miles Franklin Award (in 2007 for *Carpentaria*) and the Stella Prize (in 2018 for *Tracker*).

·

アレクシス·ライトはクイーンズランド州カーペンタリア湾の南部高地のワーニィ(Waanyi)族に属するオーストラリア作家である。ライトは、『カーペンタリア』(Carpentaria, 2006)や『スワン·ブック』(The Swan Book, 2013)などの小説を出版し、さらに『天下を取れ、この地のこの老人のように』（*Take Power Like This Old Man Here*，1998）<中央土地評議会の口述歴史本>、『グロッグ戦争』（*Grog War*，1997）<北部特別地域におけるアルコールの乱用についての研究>、そして『追跡者』（*Tracker*，2017）<先住民の指導者であった追跡者ティルマス（Tracker Tilmouth）についての回顧録>などのノンフィクションの作品を出版している。ライトの作品は海外でも、たとえば、中国、アメリカ、イギリス、インド、イタリア、フランス、ポーランドなどの国々で出版されている。現在彼女は、メルボル オーストラリア文学ボァブヴィエ・チェア（Boisbouvier Chair）に就任、オーストラリア文学の促進、発展に努める。ライトは、先住民作家として、2007 年に『カーペンタリア』でマイルズ・フランクリン賞を、そして 2018 年に『追跡者』でステラ賞を受賞した。これら二つの賞を受賞した先住民作家はライトのみである。

—

中文译者简介
About the Translator
翻訳者について

—

李尧
Li Yao
リ・ヤオ

李尧（1946—　）：资深翻译家，中国作家协会会员，北京外国语大学客座教授，澳大利亚悉尼大学荣誉文学博士（2014），西悉尼大学荣誉文学博士（2019）。
1966 年从内蒙古师范大学毕业以后，李尧在内蒙古的一家刊物做编辑和记者，直到 1992 年被中国商务部培训中心聘为英语教授。1968 年起开始文学创作，发表中短篇小说、报告文学百万字。1978 年起开始文学翻译。四十多年来翻译出版英美、澳大利亚文学、文化、历史著作 53 部，其中澳大利亚文学 32 部。长篇小说《浪子》《红线》《卡彭塔利亚湾》获澳大利亚澳中理事会翻译奖。2008 年，因其在中澳文化交流特别是翻译领域的突出贡献，澳大利亚政府授予其“杰出贡献奖章”。2018 年，在华澳大利亚研究基金会授予其“终身成就奖”。

·

Li Yao (1946—　): Visiting Professor of Australian

Studies Centre, Beijing Foreign Studies University. Doctor of Letters (honoris causa) awarded by the University of Sydney in 2014, Doctor of Letters (honoris causa) awarded by the Western Sydney University in 2019, Senior Translator.
After graduating from Inner Mongolian Normal University in 1966, Li Yao worked as a writer and editor at journals in Inner Mongolia until his appointment as Professor of English at the Training Center of the Ministry of Commerce, Beijing, in 1992. He began his literary translation career in 1978. In the past 40 years, he has translated and published 53 British, American and Australian literature, culture and history works. He became a member of the Chinese Writers' Association in 1986, specialising in literary translation. He won the Australia-China Council's inaugural Translation Prize in 1996 for *The Ancestor Game* by Alex Miller, and won it again in 2012 for *Carpentaria* by Alexis Wright, both Miles Franklin-winning novels. He was awarded the Council's Golden Medallion in 2008 for his distinguished contribution in the field of Australian literary translation in China. He was awarded Certificate of Achievement by FASIC, in recognition of his lifelong contributions to the art of translation and to bring Australian Literature to Chinese readers in 2018.

·

リ・ヤオ（1946—　）は、上級翻訳家であり、また北京外国語大学オーストラリア・センターの客員教授である。2014 年にシドニー大学、2019 年に西シドニー大学より、名誉博士号（文学）を授与された。リ・ヤオは、1966 年に内モンゴル師範大学を卒業後、内モンゴル自治区で雑誌の編集者およびライターとなる。1992 年に北京の中華人民共和国商務部の研修センターの英文学教授に就任する。1978 年より、文学作品の翻訳家としての活動を始める。彼は、過去 40 年間にわたり、

53 作にのぼる英・米・豪の文学、文化、歴史に関する作品を翻訳し出版した。1986 年に翻訳家として中国作家協会のメンバーとなった。1996 年にアレックス・ミラー（Alex Miller）の『アンセスター・ゲーム』（*The Ancestor Game*）で、豪・中カウンシル（*the Australia-China Council*）設立記念翻訳賞を受賞、2012 年にアレクシス・ライト（Alexis Wright）の『カーペンタリア』（*Carpentaria*）の翻訳で、再度同賞を受賞した。両作家ともにマイルズ・フランクリン賞受賞者である。またリ・ヤオは、翻訳を通してオーストラリア文学を中国へ紹介した功績が称えられ、豪・中カウンシルのゴールド・メダルが授与された。また彼は、中国オーストラリア研究基金（Foundation for Australian Studies in China）より、永年にわたり中国人読者にオーストラリア文学を翻訳にて紹介することに貢献したことが認められ、2018 年に達成証明書が授与された。

—

日文译者简介
About the Translator
翻訳者について

—

有满保江
Arimitsu Yasue
有満保江

有满保江，同志社大学荣誉教授。1985 年，有满保江因“寻找一个地方：帕特里克 . 怀特的早期小说中对于风景的描写以及对身份的寻找”一文获得澳大利亚国立大学硕士学位。回国后在帝塚山学院大学（1988—1995）及京都的同志社大学（1995—2014）执教英文和澳大利亚文学。去澳大利亚留学前，她翻译了一些澳大利亚和新西兰短篇小说。回日本之后，和他人合作编辑、翻译了当代澳大利亚短篇小说，以《钻石狗：当代澳大利亚短篇小说集》为题出版（现代企划室出版，2008）。这些短篇反映了当代澳大利亚社会里的多种文化并存的特色。近来她一直在参与以“现代澳大利亚文学杰作选”为主题的一个十年的翻译项目。目前为止，此项目已经翻译并出版了其中 6 本，直到完成所有 10 本书的翻译和出版。除了翻译之外，有满保江教授的主要著作有 :《澳大利亚的民族特性——从文学角度探索其变化》（东京大学出版会，2003）（该书获澳大利亚政府“尼尔 · 柯里爵士奖”特别奖），《当代澳大利亚研究 : 全球化时代的文学、历史、电影和媒体研究》（共同编著，音羽书房 · 鹤见书店，2017）等。曾任日本澳大利亚学会会长（2010—2013）、日本澳大利亚及新西兰文学会会长（2014—2018）。

Arimitsu Yasue is Professor Emeritus, Doshisha University in Kyoto. She studied at the Australian National University, and obtained master's degrees for "Finding a Place: Landscape and the Search for Identity in the Early Novels of Patrick White" in 1985. She taught English and Australian literature at Tezukayama Gakuin University in Osaka (1988—1995), and Doshisha University in Kyoto (1995—2014). She translated some Australian and New Zealand short stories into Japanese before she went to Australia. Returning to Japan, she co-edited and translated contemporary Australian short stories, which appeared as *Diamond Dog: A Collection of Contemporary Australian Short Stories* (2008). These stories reflect multicultural features of the contemporary Australian society. She is currently working on the "Ten-Year-Project" of translating contemporary Australian novels. In this project, they have published six novels and will continue until they publish ten novels all together. Besides translations, ARIMITSU is the author of the book, *Australian Identity: Struggle and Transformation in Australian Literature in* 2003 (awarded Australia-Japan Foundation Sir Neil Currie Special Prize in 2003), and co-edited *Contemporary Australian Studies: Literature, History, Film and Media Studies in a Globalizing Age* (2017). She was the president of the Australian Studies Association of Japan (2010—2013), and the president of the Australia New Zealand Literary Society of Japan (2014—2018)

有満保江（同志社大学名誉教授）：オーストラリア国立大学にて修士号取得（オーストラリア政府機関豪日交流基金の大学院奨学生として留学）。帰国後、帝塚山学院大学（1988 —1995）および同志社大学（1995—2014）にて教鞭をとる。留学前にオーストラリア文学短編集に翻訳を掲載、帰国後は『ダイヤモンド・ドッグ——多文化を映す現代オーストラリア短編小説集』共編訳（現代企画室、2008）を出版する。2012 年より「現代オ ーストラリア文学傑作選」（現代企画室主催）と題する翻訳プロジェクトに関わり、すでに 6 冊の小説の翻訳書の企画、監修に携わる。著書としては、『オーストラリアのアイデンティティー文学にみるその模索と変容』（東京大学出版会、2003），オーストラリア政府サ ー・ニールカリー賞特別賞受賞；『現代オーストラリア研究：グローバル時代における文学、歴史、フィルムとメディア研究』共編著（音羽書房・鶴見書店、2017）などがある。オーストラリア学会会長（2010 —2013）、日本オーストラリア・ニュージーランド文学会会長（2014 — 2018）を務める。

图书在版编目（CIP）数据

地平线上的奥德赛 /（澳）亚历克西斯·赖特著；（日）有满保江，李尧译．— 北京：北京联合出版公司，2021.7
ISBN 978-7-5596-5208-9

Ⅰ．①地… Ⅱ．①亚… ②有… ③李… Ⅲ．①中篇小说－澳大利亚－现代 Ⅳ．①I611.45

中国版本图书馆 CIP 数据核字 (2021) 第 061594 号

地平线上的奥德赛
作　　者：[澳]亚历克西斯·赖特
译　　者：李尧 [日]有满保江
出 品 人：赵 红 仕
策　　划：乐府文化
责任编辑：李　　伟
特约编辑：刘 衎 衎
装帧设计：[澳]莉莉·萨文克 Hamu
北京联合出版公司出版
（北京市西城区德外大街 83 号楼 9 层 100088）
北京联合天畅文化传播公司发行
北京美图印务有限公司印刷 新华书店经销

60千字 787 毫米 ×1092 毫米 1/32 印张 5.75
2021 年 7 月第 1 版 2021 年 7 月第 1 次印刷
ISBN 978-7-5596-5208-9
定价： 39.80 元